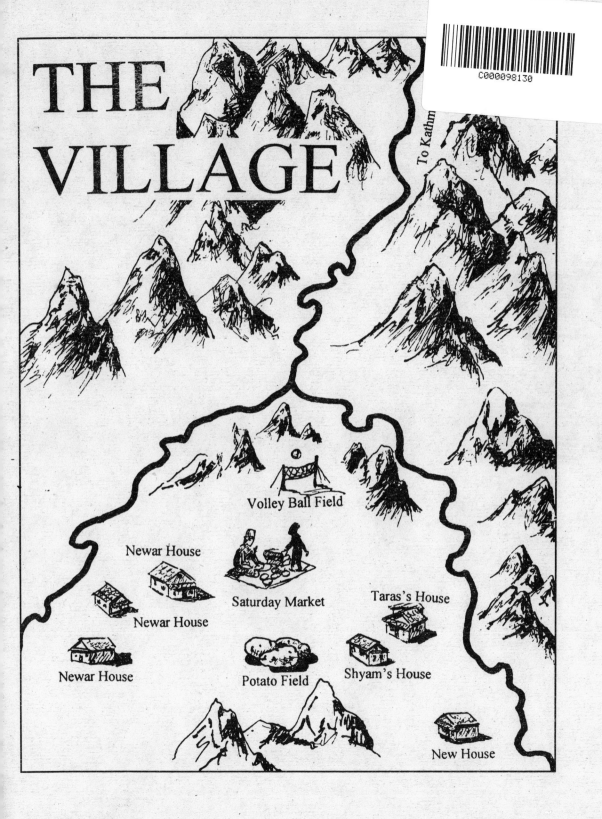

THE VILLAGE

To Kathm

Volley Ball Field

Newar House

Saturday Market

Taras's House

Newar House

Newar House

Potato Field

Shyam's House

New House

Contents

PIECES OF THE PUZZLE
The Story of Shyam and Ram

Joanne W. Stephenson

PILGRIMS PUBLISHING
Varanasi◆Kathmandu

PIECES OF THE PUZZLE
The Story of Shyam and Ram
By Joanne W. Stephenson
Illustrations by Duke Ottinger

Published by:
PILGRIMS PUBLISHING

An imprint of:
PILGRIMS BOOK HOUSE
B 27/98 A-8, Nawabganj Road
Durga Kund, Varanasi-221010, India
Tel: 91-542-314060, 312496
Fax: 91-542-314059
E-mail: pilgrims@satyam.net.in
Website: www.pilgrimsbooks.com

Distributed in India by:
PILGRIMS BOOK HOUSE
B 27/98 A-8, Nawabganj Road
Durga Kund, Varanasi-221010, India
Tel: 91-542-314060, 312496
Fax: 91-542-314059
E-mail: pilgrims@satyam.net.in
Website: www.pilgrimsbooks.com

Distributed in Nepal by:
PILGRIMS BOOK HOUSE
P O Box 3872, Thamel,
Kathmandu, Nepal
Tel: 977-1-424942
Fax: 977-1-424943
E-mail: pilgrims@wlink.com.np

ISBN 81-7769-198-8
Rs. 145.00

Edited by Kate Stephenson Todd

Printed in India

PREFACE

Pieces of the Puzzle is the story of Newar twins Ram and Shyam, one of whom spends his young adult years in the city and the other who lives in the mountains. I have tried to describe the customs of the Newar peoples in Nepal, and the differences between the Newars living in the city, and those living in the mountains. Each young man strives to find a lifestyle satisfying to his inner self. The story is based on my close association with a Newar family over a period of ten years.

This work would not have been possible without the help of Karna Bahadur Shrestha who answered all of my questionnaires about Newars living in the mountains. I would like to thank Mekh Gurung for conducting interviews; my writing group who listened patiently to each chapter; Lisa Chewning for her editorial help; my daughter, Kate Stephenson Todd who added many helpful suggestions in rewriting; Juju Tuladhar for checking for cultural accuracy; and Rama Tiwari, who continues to be an inspiration for my writing on Nepal. A special thanks to Duke Ottinger, the patient illustrator of this work.

Joanne Stephenson
Oakmont, Pennsylvania
October, 2001

Chapter One

THE POTATO HOLE

Chapter One

THE POTATO HOLE

Maya's heart gave a start when she heard the screams. The baby never cried. Maya's two children, Devi and Purna, had been running up the hill ahead of her, Devi, her five year old daughter, carrying the baby. Maya was out of breath from climbing from one terrace to the next carrying the digging tools. In Nepal the terraces are steep. The day was warm for early spring and the field for the maize was uneven from the recent plowing. Even so she quickly reached the potato field and the hole they had not finished yesterday. Devi was lying flat on her stomach, whimpering. Purna stood by helplessly. Maya grabbed the baby from the hole in the dirt. Her forehead was dripping blood. Maya deftly dabbed at the cut with the end of her sash.

"I told you not to run when you were carrying the baby. Now she will have a sore on her face for her Rice Feeding Ceremony."

"I'm sorry, Aama," Devi said.

"Run get some water from the stream over there by the next field. Purna, go start getting wood ready for the fire in the potato hole."

Maya sat down above the hole, the baby cradled in her lap. Blood continued to run from the wound as Maya put pressure on it. "Run faster, Devi," she agonized. Devi came back, her hands cupped to hold water. The water had run out. Devi looked down at her aama with tears running down her cheeks. She could not do anything right today. She had hurt their baby and now could not help. The flowing blood frightened her.

"Here, take this," Maya said as she thrust a metal cup into Devi's hand, "And hurry. Don't spill any of the water this time."

Maya continued to apply pressure. As the bleeding slowed a little she began to think about other consequences of the fall. She knew her brother would send a new outfit and a bracelet for the baby to wear for the Ceremony, which was only three days away. She wanted the baby to look perfect.

Devi returned with the water, holding a leaf over the cup to keep the water in. She was tiny for her age, and her dress hung on her. It had a few rips around the hem and now the front was covered with dirt from the fall. Devi's square face was tear-stained with streaks of mud and her shoulder-length black hair was a tangled mess. But her mother had eyes only for the baby as she dipped the end of her white sash into the water and dabbed gently at the small cut. The bleeding was slowing, but the baby continued to cry softly. Devi knelt down and stroked the baby's arms. The bleeding stopped and there were only a few sniffles.

"Devi, clean out the dirt you pushed back into the hole with your fall. Purna, start a fire."

"Why can't Ram and Shyam help us? School was out a half an hour ago," Purna said as he put a few dried cornhusks at the bottom of the hole. As he brought some wood for the fire, he had been thinking about his older twin brothers. Even though he was only seven, he enjoyed working on the farm, but he wished his older brothers would help with the hard work.

Like Devi, he was short, but he was stocky. He had changed from his school uniform and wore the *daura suruwal* that the boys in the village used to wear. He wished he had a regular shirt and pants like some of the other boys. His black burr haircut framed his round face.

"Because Shyam is helping Baa make the doors and windows for the Gurung house and Ram is getting merchandise together for the Saturday market," Maya said as she rocked the baby.

After her terrible fright, she took a deep breath and looked across the valley towards the Himalayas. She found herself thinking about the twins. Maya wished they would help, too, because she liked having them around. She was so proud of them, the fact that they were the only twins in the village and yet were each becoming distinct individuals. For that matter she wished her husband could help, too, but he had to finish up the carpentry work, so he could bring home cash; she would need to buy rice and other supplies at the Saturday market for the Rice-Feeding Ceremony. Her's was a nice family, she continued to muse. Her marriage had been arranged. Her family lived in the Ramachap District of Nepal, about six hours away by walking. She rarely saw them. Her husband had been good to her. They had not been married long before the twins arrived. He insisted she go to adult literacy classes when the boys started school so she could help with the lessons. The work on the farm

4

was hard, but she was content.

"The fire is going," Purna said.

Maya started from her reverie. "Let's let it burn a little while we start another hole over here. Baby's asleep now, so I can help," Maya said as she laid the baby gently on her shawl.

Maya and Devi started digging while Purna assembled more wood.

"Purna and Devi, go cover the first fire so it will smoulder." Maya continued to scrape the hole she was working on until it was about thirty centimeters deep. The three continued to work in this manner until there were ten holes smouldering. The soil would be well sterilized now and they could plant the potatoes soon.

"I'm cold," said Devi.

"The sun is going down," said Purna.

"Purna, you gather the tools. You are going to have to carry them because I have the baby. Devi, you help Purna," Maya said as she hoisted the baby onto her back in the shawl.

"When can I carry Baby again?" Devi said. She was afraid her mother would say, "Never."

But all she said was, "Not today."

Chapter Two

SHYAM'S JOINT

Chapter Two

SHYAM'S JOINT

You are working too slowly. When are you going to finish those window frames? You did only one yesterday. I need to get them done and the shutters made before the monsoon starts. That was Nagendra Gurung talking.

"I'll get my son to help me," Karna replied. Karna was the father of Shyam and Ram. Like other Nepali children, they called their father Baa. "Maybe we can get two done today and two tomorrow. I hope you can pay me some rupees today, though, because my wife needs to buy supplies at the Saturday market for the Rice Feeding Ceremony."

Nagendra grunted and walked over to talk to the men finishing the stone roof.

"Shyam, I want you to look at this window frame you watched me make yesterday," said Karna. "When I get done planing this board, you can make the corner joint for the next one. I'll help to begin with and then you can finish the joint while I get started on the next log."

Shyam was thrilled. He had been helping his father for several years now, mostly just bringing logs or tools to his father's workplace and holding the wood while his father worked. His fingers itched to start working on his own. He felt he knew all the processes by heart. It looked easy as he watched his father work. Shyam had heard over and over again about his Newar background and how this tribe of Nepali had excelled in woodworking and other artistic pursuits. He wanted to be part of that heritage.

They were working in front of the Gurung house Nagendra Gurung was building. The hill rose steeply behind the house to the next terrace, and, in front of the house, dropped off precipitously to the next terrace beneath their feet. The house itself was made of rock and mud, as carefully built as if it were of brick. Now men were cutting roofing rocks to uniform size. It was the

Newars' job to make the window frames that would be inserted in the spaces made by the stone masons. Shutters for the windows would be made later.

Shyam ran to get a saw, a chisel and hammer, and the metal straight edge his father always carried. Then he felt in his school bag for a pencil.

"Come on, you still have to hold this board steady for me while I plane," Karna said. "You're not a master-carpenter yet!"

"Baa, I am fifteen now and will be celebrating my Kaite Pujaa in a few months like our cousin in Solukhumbu did last year. That means I am almost an adult and I can do all of the things you can do," Shyam retorted. He remembered those boys with their shaved heads and yellow clothes. They looked so grown up.

"That's in Solukhumbu. There are only seven Newar families in this village—not enough to have that important ceremony. There would be only you. Besides our economic condition doesn't allow us to do things like that.Come, hold this board."

Father and son resembled each other as they bent over their work. Both were short and stocky. Features were strong, the nose large, the mouth full, their dark eyes receding a bit into their strong foreheads. Both had short, bristle-cut black hair. Both wore Western-style pants and a shirt purchased at the Saturday market, and jackets Karna had brought from Kathmandu. Karna wore a topi—Shyam wanted one badly, but would have to wait until next year, his father said.

"The first thing we must do is make a square cut at the end of the board," said Karna. "Draw a line across it and down the side towards you. I will hold the board while you saw." He and Baa were changing places! Shyam picked up the saw. He crouched down and worked hard to stay on the line. He was happy when his father grunted his approval.

"Here, put this in your pocket when you are not using it," Karna said as he handed him a square piece of wood. "This will measure the mark for making the cut for the joint. Place it square to the end and make a line across the board. Now, turn the measure on edge and draw a line down both sides of your first line. Next, start at the top and saw down to your line across the board. I will watch you this time." Shyam was getting hot from concentrating so hard. He wanted to show Baa he could be a master carpenter.

"Good," Karna said to Shyam's relief. "Now saw across the board down to your first cut." Karna watched as his son worked very carefully and accurately. There was no need to chisel out the corner.

"If you do them all like this, you will be a master carpenter before long. Let's hurry and get the next board ready and you can make the mate for the joint," said Karna. It seemed to take a long time to get that log down to the smooth board that would be needed. Shyam was excited to get to the next part of the joint. He would show Baa how quickly he could complete it. As soon as Baa was done with his part, Shyam grabbed the board, held it steady on his bench, and quickly made the first cut. His father nodded for him to continue. Shyam made the next marks. The saw cuts did not quite meet. He had to saw a little further on his first cut. It went crooked, but he was able to pull the block out, leaving a rough lump in the corner. He tried fitting his new cut with the one he had done before. He was crestfallen. It would not go all the way in. He grabbed the chisel and hammer and drove hard at that lump—too hard because he went right into the wall of the joint.

"It is a good thing this is the short side of the frame," said Karna as he picked up the scrap and examined it. "Make another square cut at the end, and then another joint. Work slowly this time and I won't be standing over you. I must get back to making more boards."

Shyam felt his face redden. Baa made the work look easy and Shyam had been sure he could do it right from the start. He straightened his board on the bench, marked it for the square cut, and knelt on it firmly. As he started to saw, the board moved back and forth. Kneeling wasn't enough. He had to steady it with one hand and saw with the other, but it was a successful cut. The next two cuts went all right, too, after he figured out how to hold the board steady.

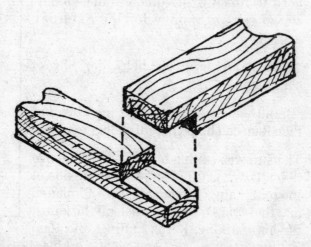

"Perfect," said Karna.

Shyam beamed.

"Now we must hurry. We must make two frames today so we can get paid. I will work on the planing while you work on the joints. The work would go much faster if Purna were here to hold boards for us, but he is busy helping your mother with the potato planting."

"Baa, I am done with my business," Ram said as he crossed the terrace and bowed to his father. He was so different from his brother. No one would have thought they were twins; Ram was tall and thin and had a more angular face, sharper nose, and black hair almost to his shoulders.

"This bamboo basket was heavy coming up the hill," Ram said as he leaned with his *doko* against a wall in front of the new house. "My teacher made me carry most of the things for the Saturday market."

"I'm glad to see you," Karna said. "Take your *doko* off and come hold this log for me while I plane. The work will go much faster. We need to finish two window frames today, so we can get money for the Saturday market."

"What about me? I need help, too," Shyam complained.

"Do all your measuring and marking and then Ram can help you," his father rejoined.

The sun was setting behind the hill above them. It was getting darker on their side of the mountain. The boards were all planed and they were trying to finish off the joints, Shyam marking, Karna cutting, and Ram holding. Ram never liked woodworking, but he realized his father was in a bind. Besides, they would have more money to spend at the Saturday market.

Nagendra Gurung was standing off to one side, watching the whole operation. To him, it seemed the work was going slowly, yet he marveled at how the men could make something like a window frame out of a tree. He hoped he could get them to do some carving on the doorposts.

"Here's a few extra rupees for today's work. I hope you can get two more frames done tomorrow," said Nagendra.

I'll miss the Saturday market, thought Karna. *I know Shyam will help and maybe Purna can help hold*. He stuffed the money in his pocket. Ram shouldered his *doko* while Karna and Shyam gathered up the tools.

Chapter Three

THE SATURDAY MARKET

Chapter Three

THE SATURDAY MARKET

I have a new accounting system I want to show you after we get done laying out the merchandise, said Ram's math teacher as he shook and laid his end of the blue plastic tarp on the ground.

"Can't you tell me now? I know we need to keep better track of how much we sell," replied Ram.

"We'll lay out the merchandise first so we'll be ready when customers come. All the merchants around us are almost set up and I can see people beginning to gather on the terrace up there."

Ram could see the lines of shops spreading out around him, most of them on their way to being set up. He reached down to the bottom of his *doko* to get the exercise books and made a neat pile at the corner. This would help hold down that corner of the tarp. The wind might come up later. Next to them he placed a bunch of pencils after bundling them in a rubber band. The teacher began pulling things out of the other *doko* and handed them to Ram. Next came the flashlights and batteries. Ram lined up the bins of rice and tea and lentils at the back with the candy in front while his teacher set up the scales. Cigarette wrappers and tobacco were at the edge near the shoppers. The smell was already wafting into the air. Then came the things to wear—flip-flops, shoes, plastic bracelets, yarn to braid in the hair, and bolts of material at the far end. Ram stood up and went to the customer's side to see how it looked. He thought the setup looked good even with the increase in merchandise. There seemed to be no end to the things his math teacher could find to sell.

The teacher leaned over and picked up the top exercise book and opened it to the first page.

"Here, make a list of all of the merchandise we have here," said the teacher. "Then see if you can put it in alphabetical order."

This is going to take a long time, thought Ram. *I don't want to miss talking to the customers.* The excited voices of the early shoppers were escalating already. He wondered how this was going to make things better.

"Now you will put a mark beside the name of each item as you sell it. After four marks you can draw a diagonal across to indicate five, like this," the teacher said as he demonstrated. "Put the price over to the right. At the end of the day we will know how much of each thing we sold," explained the teacher.

"I wish we could write down the price of each item, but here everyone bargains and the cost will be different each time," said Ram. He liked math and would like to figure out just how much money they took in. He guessed they would just have to estimate.

Ram and the teacher sat cross-legged behind their completed shop. Ram helped every week; he was lucky his teacher would allow him to work. He liked talking with people and learning about the business. His math skills were good, so he could make change and keep track of the sales. It was interesting learning about the merchandise. Ram hoped he would have his own market some day and maybe go to Kathmandu to open a shop.

The crowds were coming. Ram smiled when he saw his mother and sister at the top of the hill. Aama carried Baby as Devi danced her way down the hill. He was always proud when his family came to see him. Today he would have a surprise for his mother. They came down the hill past the men from India selling pots and pans. He laughed when he saw Devi put her face right up to one of the pans and grin at her reflection. Now that they were on level ground, Aama handed Baby to Devi. Ram was glad Devi was given another chance to take care of their sister. He saw Aama stop to talk to the tailor who was sitting on the ground with his sewing machine. Ram had always marveled at how the tailor was able to crank the sewing machine with one hand and push the material through with the other. He wondered if Aama was ever going to stop talking and come his way.

After the tailor, his mother headed right for Ram, by-passing the meat shop and all of the others. She was smiling at him and there was a sparkle in her eyes. She seemed oblivious to Devi's entreaties to stop at other places. Soon, Aama was standing in front of him. Ram bowed to her quickly.

"Let me see that blue material with flowers over there," Maya said to Ram. "I need a new sari."

"Aama, look at this red material with gold dots in it. It would be perfect for Baby at the Rice Feeding Ceremony," Ram said. "We got it especially for you."

"But I think Uncle will bring an outfit for Baby," said Maya. "I guess we could put it aside for the next holiday. This material is pretty and the outfit could be made to fit Baby."

The bright color was dazzling in the sunlight, but Ram knew Aama could not afford both the sari and the red material.

"You could wear your old blue sari and get a new blouse for it," Ram suggested. Maya handed him the red material. Ram measured out what he thought would be enough material for Baby's new outfit along with a length of blue for the blouse for her sari.

"I want red for my dress, too," Devi said excitedly. "I want the same as Baby."

"No, you must have something different. What about this with the pink and yellow flowers?" Maya replied.

Devi hitched Baby a little further up on her hip. She pushed her lower lip out. "I guess that will be all right."

"Ram, give me a packet of tea and one manna of rice. Let me smell the tea first. Do you or your teacher have a coin I can use for the ceremony?"

"Here take this one," said the math teacher as he took a one rupee coin out of his vest pocket and handed it to her. She tucked it carefully away in her sash as she took out some notes to pay Ram.

"How much do I owe?" Maya asked.

Ram turned to his teacher, "How much should I charge?"

"Well. The rice is usually ten rupees, and the tea thirty. Let's make it 230 rupees altogether," replied the math teacher.

"I'll count it out for you," said Ram. As he took her money, she watched him and marveled at how he could count the money so fast and record the sale carefully in the exercise book at the same time.

Meanwhile, Devi was struggling with the heavy, wiggling baby.

"Here, I will take Baby," said Maya. She wrapped Baby in her shawl, tied her firmly to her back, and then took her change and the purchases.

"Don't forget to invite the other Newars who are here to the Rice Feeding Ceremony," Ram said as his mother headed back through the crowds. Devi stayed close to her mother as Aama stopped to ask Newar friends to come to the Rice Feeding Ceremony. He could imagine the conversation:

"Where did Baby get that sore on her forehead?" would be the constant question. Devi would look down at her feet as her mother told the story.

"What a shame with the Rice Feeding Ceremony coming up in a few days," would be the usual response.

He knew Devi was glad when they reached the tailor. She did not want to think about yesterday anymore. Maya handed the tailor the material and settled on a price.

"Ram, here's some money for the tailor. On your way home tonight pick up my blouse, Baby's outfit and Devi's dress to bring home. Try to get home in time to help with the potato field," Maya said as she handed him the money. Ram watched them head up the hill at a rapid pace so they could get to work. He knew she wanted to finish the potato holes this afternoon.

Chapter Four

THE RICE FEEDING CEREMONY

Chapter Four

THE RICE FEEDING CEREMONY

I win, said Shyam when Ram dropped the Lali-guras bud with which they were playing Coq. They had been playing with the remains of a red blossom Devi had been eating. This time of year children liked to eat the large flowers that bloomed on trees growing by the stream. Shyam didn't like the taste himself, but then, Devi was only five. In Coq each player bounced a stone or

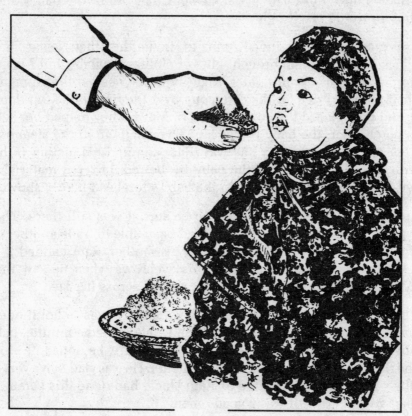

other object in the air with his heel and then bounced it toward the other player. Shyam liked to play the game with Lali-guras because a blossom hurt less than a stone when it hit his leg, and besides, he liked the green and red color. Ram and Shyam enjoyed playing the game together. They felt lucky to have each other.

"Stop your game, now," said Maya. "Ram Uncle is coming up the hill. Shyam, go help him with his heavy load. He has come all of the way from Ramachap District this morning."

Maya and Ram Uncle bowed to each other, as she took the package from her brother. Ram watched her unwrap it. The outfit was of blue, Maya's favorite color. She felt badly having to put it aside now, but Baby had on her new red outfit, appropriate for the ceremony. Then she unwrapped a heavy bracelet and clamped it on the baby's ankle. It was a custom that would bring her good luck and help to straighten her leg as she grew. Ram was glad he had bought one yesterday for the other leg with his earnings from the Saturday Market.

Now they could begin the ceremony. It would be nice to call Baby something other than "Baby" now. The priest thought that Sashi, the name the family had chosen, would be all right.

Ram was glad he had reminded Aama to invite the other Newar families in the village. Some of them brought gifts of clothes for Baby, but Maya would have to put them aside until later. Right now she needed the women's help. They had prepared rice for the ceremony over the fire on the top floor of the house, and now placed the bowl in front of Maya. They helped her get seated on the porch floor, the baby in her lap. The smells from the steaming bowl made her notice how hungry she was. Ram admired his mother in her blue sari with the new blouse and the baby in the red-flowered material he had selected. He noticed that the cut on the baby's forehead hardly showed.

Ram fingered the coin in his pocket to be sure it was still there. The silver coin was a surprise for his mother; he had been able to trade another coin for it at the Saturday market. At a nod from his mother, Ram handed it to Ram Uncle. Ram noticed his uncle raised his eyebrows when he saw the silver coin. Maya gave a start and then a smile spread across her face.

Ram Uncle scooped a bit of rice onto the coin, but it was so hot it burned his finger and the coin fell into the bowl. Ram Uncle waited a minute, fished out the coin with a leaf and wiped it off. On the next try, he hoped he would not drop the rice before he reached the baby's mouth. He was glad Maya was holding the baby's mouth open. As often as Ram Uncle had done this ceremony, the baby had always cried. It was a good omen.

24

"Aama, can we serve tea to everyone?" Ram said as he bowed to his mother. "I know there are a lot of people with our Newar friends, but I wanted to talk about going to Kathmandu." He watched his mother's face change from a contented smile to bewilderment. He could not understand her confusion. They had discussed the possibility that he might leave home. Ram guessed she had hoped he would change his mind. She liked having her children around her.

"We'll have tea," Maya said simply. How could she refuse a request of help from her son? The women rushed into the house to get the tea started while the men sat around on the courtyard walls telling jokes and making plans for planting maize.

Shyam was upset when he overheard Ram's request. He sat off by himself. He had to think. Ram had talked about opening his own shop, but Shyam had always thought it would be at the Saturday market. *I cannot remember Ram mentioning anything about Kathmandu. How can we separate? Who will I talk to about my problems now? Who will play Coq with me? Who will come help when Baa and I get busy? Purna is too small. I am committed to learning Baa's trade. I love the work, the feel of the wood, and I feel I am mastering the tools. I want to create beautiful things for my village.*

Shyam's reveries ended abruptly.

"I want to go to Kathmandu and open a store," Ram said. His father and Ram Uncle frowned. He knew he should not interrupt, but he was anxious after spending a sleepless night. Everyone stopped talking. It was Ram's turn to be startled. *Everyone was listening!* He described the work he had been doing for his math teacher and how he wanted to do more business so he could help his family.

"My brother has just opened a new, bigger store in Kathmandu and needs someone to help," a friend of Karna's said.

"Do you think he would hire me? Where could I live?" His questions came quickly. He was thankful he was being taken seriously by these adult men. Now he was ready to go and he wanted all the details settled. But his father and Ram Uncle started to laugh nervously at Ram's eagerness. He hoped they would not stop his plans.

"I am sure you could live with him," Karna's friend replied. "He has a big house and could use some extra help there, too."

Ram could see some of the other men nod in approval. He looked at Shyam's crestfallen face.

25

"I think you need to wait another year until you are old enough to be of Brataman age and have your School Leaving Certificate," his father and Ram Uncle said at once. Ram had to wait for a ceremony he would never be able to take part in?

"I know I will need my School Leaving Certificate if I am going into business, but I don't see why I need to be a year older," Ram said. He almost wished he had not said that. He thought he was acting old enough.

Fortunately, the women began passing glasses of tea and the tension seemed to relax a bit. The men started talking about crops again. Sashi was smiling happily in her mother's lap. Ram was relieved. No one had said, "No!" He looked again at Shyam's face. He would miss his brother. They relied much on each other, but he knew Shyam would never leave the village.

Chapter Five

BHAKTAPUR

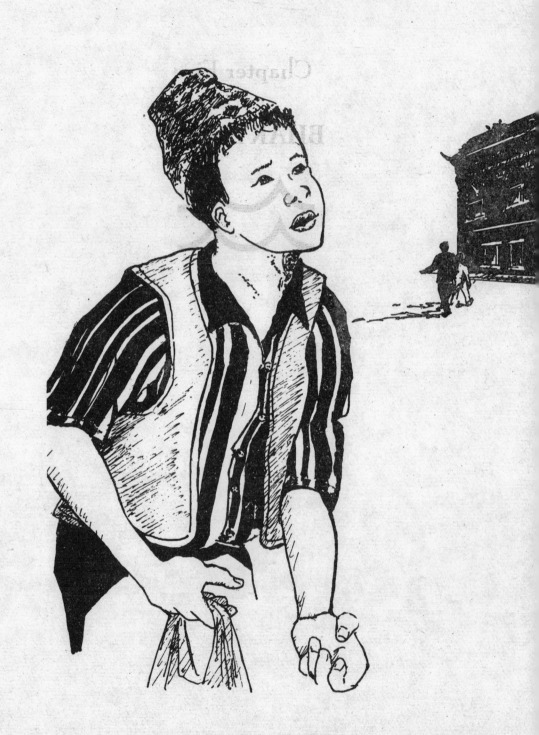

Chapter Five

BHAKTAPUR

Ram's fears came to nought. When Karna realized Ram was determined to leave, he supported him in his decision and began to help him prepare for being away from home. Ram's father had been to Kathmandu before, but the boys had been only across the valley. In the year that followed, Karna and the two boys spent much time in conversation about the differences they would find in the big city. Ram was an eager listener. Shyam was curious about the big city, but remained quiet for the most part. The city did not interest him.

"Now we must get a bus to Bhaktapur," Baa said. Ram and Shyam were so overcome by the honking cars and taxis and yelling people at the Kathmandu bus station. They could hardly hear what Baa was saying. "Pick up your *dokos*. I think the bus to Bhaktapur will come across the street," Baa shouted.

"Bhaktapur?" said Ram. "Where's Bhaktapur?"

"About a half an hour from here by bus," Baa replied

"But I thought I was going to Kathmandu. I want to work in Kathmandu and become a business man. I don't want to be a half an hour away," Ram replied. These were not the plans he had understood. What could he do?

"Come on. I see a bus coming," Baa interjected. Karna noticed Ram biting his lip and hanging his head.

"I don't want to get on that bus," Ram said in a quavering voice.

Karna had much on his mind now trying to get them to their destination, but he knew he must try to explain to his son. He let that bus pass. He was sure there would be another soon.

"Bhaktapur is a city, too. Not as big as Kathmandu, but still there is plenty of business there. Besides we have made all of the arrangements for you to stay with a Newar family and to work in their business, all for free. You are a lucky boy."

"I'm not a boy. I am a man," replied Ram. "I want to work in Kathmandu."

"You need to get more experience first. Then you can work in Kathmandu. Now you will be staying with a good Newar family who will ease the way for you and teach you many things about Newar traditions. Newars are merchants, and by living with them you will be right where you should be," Baa concluded.

"Here comes another bus. This one isn't so crowded. Push your *dokos* onto the bus and climb in afterwards." Baa considered the subject closed.

Shyam held his breath in awe as they walked through the brick-paved Durbar Square in Bhaktapur. Buildings were built of brick and wood, the most beautiful woodcarvings adorning the windows and doorways. He was rushed past the gilded copper gate of the Palace and the life-sized statue of one of the Mallas. But he stopped in his tracks when he saw the Palace of fifty-five Windows. Heavy intricate carving adorned every window. He was inspired. He knew there were not such large pieces of wood in his village, but he tried to imprint on his mind some parts of the carving to use on posts and doorways. He wanted his village to be a showplace, too.

"Namaste!" The booming voice came from a tall, heavy-set man. He wore a topi, but otherwise he had on Western garb with coat and dress shirt. He was swarthy, unusual for a Newar. "You must be Ram," he said as he grasped Ram's hand. I have been looking for you. Is this your father?"

Ram felt intimidated by this large man, but he managed a bow and a reply.

"Yes, he is my father and that is my twin brother Shyam over there looking at the windows."

"Namaste!" he said as he bowed to Baa and then shook hands. Shyam joined them and bowed before shaking hands. He was able to catch a last glimpse of the windows as they hurried down an alleyway on the other side of the square, and then burst into a light, bright courtyard. It was not a courtyard of one house, but of many. Whole families were sitting on steps of the different buildings surrounding the square.

All of them ran together, making them seem like one house. Shyam marveled at the three stories and the tile roofs. Each had three large windows across the front. Shyam hoped he could find pencil and paper to make sketches of the simple ornamentation.

It was a friendly place, with children running around. Older men were sitting around and talking while women watched the children and did laundry in the large sunken concrete enclosure across the way. One woman was washing her hair under the tap. Shyam watched another woman hang her Newari sari out an upstairs window; some of the women were wearing the black sari with the red flounce on the bottom, typical of the Newars.

Ram could not take in much of the scene now: he was too anxious about his own fate. He learned that the man's name was Surya Tuladhar, but otherwise could not understand the conversation with his father. Surya spoke in a strange language. Apparently, Baa understood, although he answered in the Nepali language of their village. Ram and Shyam followed the two men into the house and on up to the first floor. They were awe struck by the large room furnished with a colorful carpet, a soft couch and big soft chairs the likes of which the boys had not seen before, some tables, a glass-fronted cabinet full of interesting things, and most wondrous of all, a box with flashing pictures in front. Shyam noticed a packet of exercise books on top of the television. His fingers were itching to sketch what he had seen.

All were smiling as Surya introduced his family and a few neighbors. Surya's wife made an effort to talk to the boys, but could speak only in Newari. The boys tried to smile their good wishes. Shyam tapped one of the children on the shoulder and pointed to the exercise books. Luckily, the boy understood, and found a partly used book for Shyam.

Ram noticed someone putting food onto the table at the end of the room. At least the food was familiar: dal-bhat (the lentils and rice they ate at home), and curried vegetables like their mother fixed in the summer time. The chicken smelled so good!

"We have chicken only on feast days at home," Shyam whispered to Ram.

The men filled their plates first. The women would eat later, just as at home. Ram and Shyam sat together on the floor since there were not enough chairs. Ram noticed they could eat with their hands. Everyone was speaking Newari; Ram and Shyam not understanding a word. Ram was wondering if he was going to have to converse with himself for the rest of his life. At least for now, he and his brother could whisper together. As they talked, Shyam was busy trying to sketch some of the wood carvings he had seen that afternoon

"I think Baa and you are going to spend the night here before catching the bus in the morning," Ram said.

"How did you figure that out?" Shyam replied.

"Surya's wife keeps pointing to the couch and the floor and Baa keeps pointing to his watch and raising five fingers, showing you have to leave at five o'clock. Baa seems to understand the Newari, although he is not speaking it," Ram concluded.

All of a sudden it dawned on the boys that they would not see each other again for a long time. Both Ram and Shyam were silent now as they thought of the separation ahead. They had never been away from each other before. Ram broke the silence.

"I will be lonely with no one to talk to when you leave"

Shyam could do nothing but shake his head.

Chapter Six

THE STORE

Chapter Six

THE STORE

Are they talking about me? Ram wondered. Ram leaned against a keg of nails watching Surya talk with several other men who had come in as soon as he had rolled up the gate and unlocked the store. Once in a while Surya would point to Ram and then motion as if Ram was to join them. Ram edged forward a few steps as the men continued their lively banter in Newari. He tried to look bright and alert, but, other than their periodic glances, they weren't paying attention to him anyway. Ram felt silly just standing there, but he did not know what else to do. Edging closer with Surya's motions only made him uncomfortable.

A young boy came in with a carrier full of glasses of tea. That was a welcome relief. He counted the glasses—six—so maybe he would get one, too. The boy gave one to each of the men in turn and offered the last one to Ram. Ram was relieved. At least he could concentrate on the warm sweet tea instead of his own awkwardness. The men continued to talk and gesture as they sipped their tea. After a while they returned their glasses to the rack, clasped hands, nodded at Ram, and filed out the door.

"Why didn't you come closer and talk with us?" Surya said with a scowl. He turned from the door and came over to face Ram.

"I couldn't understand a word they said," Ram said. "How could I respond? In our village we speak only Nepali. Didn't you notice last night how Baa responded in Nepali, although he understood what you said?" said Ram.

"Well, you had better learn Newari quickly. It's the Newari language that makes us Newar and you are a Newar," Surya replied in Nepali.

Ram felt a lump rising in his throat. The difference between the Newars in his village and the Newars in Bhaktapur was a new and disturbing discovery for

Ram. He felt overwhelmed, but Surya kept talking.

"Help me take these pots and pans outside so people can see what we have for sale," said Surya. "I'll take this stack, and you get the one over there. Be sure not to drop any because it will dent the pot." Ram was so happy to have something to do at last that he moved too quickly and one of the pots wiggled loose. Shame-faced, Ram bent to pick up the pot and dropped all the rest. Surya just shook his head as he helped Ram stack them neatly outside.

"Come on, we need to restock these bins," said Surya. With that, Surya picked up a large carton of screws. Ram rushed to pick up the box next to it.

"No! No! Only one bin at a time. Otherwise we will get confused," Surya said as he started back to the bin marked "screws". Ram, red-faced, followed Surya. Surya put the box on the floor, opened it, and took out a handful of screws. Ram reached in with both hands, dropping several on the floor.

"Dropping them on the floor is not getting them into the bin," Surya snarled. "If you can't do things right, you shouldn't do them at all."

The whole day went like that. He wished he had counted the times he heard, *If you can't do things right, don't do them at all.* Why did he do so well with his math teacher at the Saturday Market, but he could do nothing right here? At least things were better when a customer came in. For a few minutes he did not hear, *If you can't do things right, don't do them at all.* He was intrigued when Surya used the cash drawer. He knew he would be good at that. Every time he tried to take the customer's money, though, Surya would step in front of him. In frustration, Ram picked up a broom and started sweeping.

"Don't sweep while a customer is in the store," Surya said. It seemed that Ram could do nothing but stand and look helpless. He felt like the poor, stupid boy that Surya was making him out to be. There was nothing he could say or do to improve his image.

At least Surya was speaking Nepali except when a Newar came in. But Ram was intimidated, and was afraid to speak at all.

Would the day never end?

Ram did not say a word as they trudged home at eight o'clock. Surya greeted friends in Newari, but otherwise he was silent, too. They passed several other hardware stores in the neighborhood, some clothing stores, a wood carving shop, some women selling groceries along the street...His father had been right. There was a lot of business in Bhaktapur.

Ram kept trying to reconstruct the day and figure out how to please. The harder he had tried to please, the worse things became. Somehow he was going to have to learn Newari, but he did not know where to begin. In the village, everyone talked and they understood one another. And now he had to face a whole houseful of people who could not or would not speak his language. They were kind, but not aware of his needs. He wished he could talk to Shyam.

Chapter Seven

A DAY OFF

Chapter Seven

A DAY OFF

Ram could hardly distinguish one day from the next. Get up. Drink tea. Walk to work with Surya. Try to please Surya at work. Walk home. Eat. Sit on the steps. Watch the neighbors for a few minutes. Wonder who the girl was sitting across the way. Go to bed.

On the way to work Surya always kept pointing to things, expecting Ram to say what they were in Newari. He was trying to learn just a few words at a time, but Surya never repeated any words. New words kept coming and the Newars spoke so fast that Ram could not follow. Surya always ran out of patience.

"Won't you ever learn? How can you expect to become a businessman if you can't speak the language? And, then at night you don't say anything."

"That's because no one speaks slow enough for me to understand," Ram replied. "At the store at least some people who come in speak Nepali. They seem glad that I can talk with them."

"I should stop speaking Nepali to you altogether. Then you will have to learn."

This sort of conversation went on every day. At times a lump would rise in his throat as he thought about Shyam and the rest of his family and how easy it had been with them. He wished he could talk to Shyam.

"This is Saturday," Ram said. He surprised himself and used the Newari word for Saturday. Surya did not even notice. "I see that some of the stores close on Saturday. Why don't we?" continued Ram.

"Lots of people need to buy hardware on their days off," Surya replied. "Besides you don't have anything else to do."

Ram was quiet and started thinking about the girl across the square. He found out her name was Chandra. He would like to spend more time talking with her. She went to school unlike a lot of girls in his village who had to stay home and help. If he were off on a Saturday maybe she could teach him Newari.

"Maybe on a Saturday someone could sit down with me and teach me Newari," Ram responded. Ram saw that Surya was considering; Surya was moving his lips as if talking to himself.

"Why don't you take Saturday morning off," Surya said aloud. "I'll speak to Indra across the square. He goes to school and has Saturdays off, too. Perhaps he can get some Newari into your head."

Not all that Ram had hoped for, but it was a start.

On the next Saturday Ram was up early to take his weekly bath. He put on his one clean shirt, brushed his hair and tried to wipe the dust off his shoes. He was having a hard time trying not to look his usual glum self as he drank his tea. Surya's wife smiled at him. Today was bound to be better, Ram thought.

Chandra was sitting on her steps chattering with one of her friends. Ram could not understand her. What was he to do?

"Excuse me," he said.

She looked up, smiling at him brightly. It was the warmest smile he had seen in the six weeks he had been here. Her hair hung down over her dark eyes and over the shoulders of her lavender-flowered surawal khotaa. The kothaa hung gracefully over her slim body. Red sandals peeked out from under the surawal. Ram was quiet for a moment, he was so taken with her beauty close-up.

"Can you help me learn Newari?" he asked timidly in Nepali. He breathed a sigh of relief—she seemed to understand as she tilted her head towards him. Chandra considered for a minute and then pushed her long black hair behind her ears; she continued to smile at him. Ram smiled back, shyly.

"Maybe my brother can help you. He's studying to be a teacher. He can help us both. I need to learn the writing and the grammar and then you can help me with Nepali."

"Surya gave me the day off today, A Ram replied, "so I want to start my lessons now."

On that first day Indra worked with Ram to teach him just a few sentences he could use right away, "My name is Ram." "Today is Saturday." "May I help you? "That pan costs—rupees."

"Practice these four sentences every day," Indra instructed. "Also you must learn all the days of the week and the numbers one to ten. We will meet again Wednesday night to see how you are doing, and give you some more work."

"Where is Chandra? I thought she was going to take lessons, too," Ram said.

"She has to help with the cooking. Besides she knows this beginning stuff. She has always spoken Newari with the family. When we get to the writing, maybe she can join us," Indra replied.

"Today is Saturday. My name is Ram," Ram said as he stood in front of Chandra on the steps.

Chandra laughed and clapped her hands. "Now, tell me how you say it in Nepali." Chandra imitated him perfectly. Of course, she had to speak Nepali in school every day. Ram wished he could speak as fast in Newari as she could in Nepali. Ram worked hard at his lessons, more to hear Chandra's praise then to be able to speak Newari. At least Surya thought he was making enough progress to let him have Saturday mornings off and let him go early Wednesday nights. Ram knew his numbers well after only two weeks. It felt good to respond in Newari when some one asked the price. Chapu for one, nipu for two, sopu, pepu, nhapu, instead of the ek, dui, tin, char, pach of the Nepali. The differences were daunting.

"Now that you know numbers, maybe I can start teaching you how to use the cash register," Surya said. Ram was pleased, but he knew there would be much insistence on doing things a certain way and a few more lessons in *If you can't do things right, it's better not to do them at all*. Ram was happy that he had finally conquered some of the needed Newari. It helped in the store and in talking with Chandra.

But Ram was still having trouble pleasing Surya. Ram was too eager to voice his own ideas and hurried through tasks so fast that he made mistakes. *If you can't do things right, it's better not to do them at all*. Ram was beginning to think Surya's criticism reflected on Ram's rural background. He knew Surya was wondering if Ram would ever learn and ir it would be easier for him to work by himself. The last thing Ram wanted was to have to go back to the village.

If you can't do things right, it's better not to do them at all. Ram was ready to not do them at all. He thought Surya's methods were not the best even though he was supposed to respect Surya and do as he said. Ram longed to talk with Shyam and his father to see what they thought about what he was doing. Even though he could speak more with Chandra now, he needed his family. Dashain was two months away. He hoped Surya would let him go home for the two week holiday.

Chapter Eight

GAAI JATRA

Chapter Eight

GAAI JATRA

No work today, Surya announced over their morning tea. "Why not?" Ram asked. "Haven't you heard people talk about Full Moon Day or Lentil Day? All Newars celebrate this one. We'll have a big feast tonight out in the square. I went out early this morning and bought a goat. I want you to help me slaughter him."

Ram could not believe that there was yet another Newar feast to be celebrated. This time at least he should be able to take part. He had helped his father kill a goat at Dashain last year, so he knew what to do. He took the khukuri knife his father had given him and went outside to sharpen it.

"Let me feel your knife," Surya said when he came out with his knife. "That's not near sharp enough to skin a goat. *If you can't do it right, it's not worth doing at all.* You come in and get me when you think it's sharp enough and we'll go slaughter the goat. The women need the goat's meat so they can start cooking."

Ram was almost in tears. He thought he had done a good job. Would Surya never be satisfied? He tried to hide his feelings as he bent to work on the edges once again. Surya came out again.

"I can't wait any longer. You will have to do the best you can with that dull knife. Untie the goat and bring him around to the back of the house."

Ram picked up his knife, untied the goat, and followed Surya. Soon, the two men returned carrying the goat dripping with blood. They took him over to the far corner of the courtyard to finish the job. Some other men came out to help and the goat's meat was soon ready for the women to cook. Since this was Lentil Day, other women would be working on a dish of lentils and beans. Later they would cook  the rice. It seemed as if each family was trying to outdo the next with food. Ram's stomach was yearning for something to eat. The smells were almost overpowering. The other men were just lazing around and talking, but Ram was more interested in watching the women. Once in a while he caught a glimpse of Chandra, who was helping with the rice.

Finally food. Ram ate and ate and ate. It had been a long wait. But already the clouds were gathering for the afternoon monsoon rain. As the drenching rain drove at them, everyone grabbed plates and pots of food and dashed for cover. At least it might cool things off a bit.

Ram sat with the family. They started talking about *Gaai Jatra* coming the next day and then *Indra Jatra* would follow and after that Dashain. Ram didn't know about *Gaai Jatra*, but he said he had heard of *Indra Jatra*. Indra, who had come in with them, chimed in,

"I bet *Indra Jatra* in your village isn't as much fun as it is here. After all I am named after the god. He's known for his bravery as well as being a god of rain and food grain."

Ram was afraid to admit he had only heard of Indra Jatra, but had never celebrated it.

"Dashain is my favorite holiday," Ram exclaimed. "I hope I get to go home for it."

"The rain has stopped," Indra said. "Let's go outside and dance. I'll go get my drum." Chandra and her friends gathered on steps and started singing. Arms and legs began churning to the beat of the drum. Even Surya smiled, although he didn't take part in the dancing. Ram had never danced before, but soon found himself out with the crowd. They danced some in the village, but he and Shyam had never taken part. He thought Shyam would enjoy this

"Hurry up with that sweeping," said Surya. As Ram was reaching with his broom, he knocked over a stack of pans with a clatter. Ram tried to close his ears to the inevitable *if you can't do it right, don't do it at all.* He was ready to put his broom down and leave the store.

"Here, I will help you pick them up," Surya said to Ram's surprise and relief. "Then sweep down the middle while I close out the cash drawer. We need to hurry so we can go celebrate *Gaai Jatra.*"

"What is *Gaai Jatra?*" Ram asked.

Surya was remarkably patient as he explained.

"On a certain date right around this time of year the gates of the kingdom were closed and therefore anyone who died after that date could not get into heaven. The cow was able to open one of the gates with its horns so the dead could go through."

"But how do they celebrate *Gaai Jatra?*" Ram persisted.

"Weren't you listening at home? On the day of the festival, families of someone who has died send out boys in the guise of cows. The cows are worshiped in the house and then the boys take to the streets and everyone enters into the festivities. Sometimes other mask-wearers are out there, too, mostly just to add to the fun. There is lots of music.

"Haven't you been listening at home? Didn't you know what they were talking about?" Surya asked. "Don't you celebrate it in your village?" Surya didn't wait for a response. "You wait and see. You will enjoy it. My wife is making a cow mask for you."

Ram couldn't help but get caught up in the excitement as they walked quickly through the streets toward home. Surya's wife hurried toward them with two masks, one for each of them. Ram laughed as he put his on. This would be fun. He got into an informal line behind Surya and found himself dancing through the streets. He thought he heard Chandra's giggle behind one of the masks. Buddhists and non-Newar Hindus were clapping and urging the dancers on.

In these two days Ram had more fun than he had had since he came to Bhaktapur. It had been a double holiday. Holidays were joyous occasions and there were so many of them here. *Why weren't there more in the village? Ram wondered. It would be a way of getting away from the grinding work of living. I guess the people in the village are too poor and there isn't time that time of year.*

It had been a good evening for Ram, and he thought he was going to enjoy living in the city. If only he were doing better at the store. He knew the next day it would be back to *If you can't do it right, it's not worth doing.* Ram was beginning to wonder if the fault all lay with him. He was anxious to get out on his own and see what he could do.

Chapter Nine

HOME FOR DASHAIN?

Chapter Nine

HOME FOR DASHAIN?

I want to go home for Dashain, Ram blurted out on their way to work the next morning.

"But you were having so much fun the last two days. I thought you would want to celebrate the big festival with us. And besides, our store can't close for two weeks. I need you."

Ram was finding himself desperate to go home. He needed the two weeks off from *if you can't do it right, it's not worth doing*. Ram liked the excitement of the city, but he longed for the familiarity of his village and his family. He felt he had learned a lot about business in the city, but he thought Surya should be doing things differently. Bins could be put in a better order so customers could find what they wanted and so he could restock the shelves more than one box at a time. Picture labels could be put around the store, so even those who could not read could find things. He and his math teacher had better order at the Saturday market. If he went home, he was sure his math teacher and his father and Shyam could help him figure out what he should do.

Ram began formulating a plan in his mind about how to get Surya to allow him to go home for the holiday. For the next weeks Ram worked hard on his Newari. He got Indra to spend their tutoring time just talking, mostly about the holiday and all of its customs. For once, with this holiday, there was not such a difference between the village and the city. The best part about these sessions was that Chandra was taking part. She seemed to enjoy these more informal sessions. It was fun being able to talk to her in her own language.

His new understanding helped at home, too. He was beginning to follow what Surya's wife said. The children in their household suddenly made sense instead of yammering like a bunch of magpies. Ram hoped that if he learned to talk with Surya and the family in the evenings they would understand his need to go home for the Dashain Festival.

Soon, Ram found himself studying Surya as a person rather than as an adversary. Even though they did not get home from the store until after eight o'clock, Surya always went looking for his children, greeting them with a smile. He seemed to have true affection for them. While his wife was completing preparation of the evening meal, Surya would sit with his son and daughter talking about their school work. His daughter obviously enjoyed sitting close to her father, looking up at him with adoring eyes. Surya insisted on going over their homework with them. Unfortunately, his daughter was called on often to help with the dinner.

"This writing is a mess. If you can't do it right, it is not worth doing. Rewrite it!" Surya said to his son. Ram was secretly glad Surya's son was receiving the same treatment as he had. "Two plus three is not four," Surya said to his small daughter. "Fix it! If you can't do it right, it's not worth doing." Her eyes began to well up with tears and her father gave her a tender pat on the back as she ran off to fix her error.

Both children returned quickly with their corrected work, bowing and presenting it to their father. Surya nodded his approval.

"Next time do it right the first time. If you can't do it right, it's not worth doing," Surya said as he dismissed them with a smile. "Go get some candles. The power is supposed to go off tonight, "Surya said as he handed his son a few rupees. "Go help your mother, A he said to his daughter.

Ram could see that Surya was almost as firm and exacting with his children as he had been with him. There was no discussion there as to why two plus three was not four. Surya required unquestioning obedience and yet there was a certain tenderness there.

Some weeks later Ram found his moment. It was one of the few nights Surya's wife sat with the family to eat.

"I haven't seen my family for six months," Ram began in Newari.

"You're not starting on that Dashain business again, are you?" snarled Surya.

"I think Dashain should be spent with the family," Surya's wife interjected quickly. "We visit our parents and our children are all around us. Ram is not part of our family. I think he should go home. Ram is young and this is his first time away. He needs to be with his family." Surya's wife fell silent and looked directly at her husband.

Surya's wife spoke very little in mixed company, but Ram had noticed that Surya usually listened. Surya closed his eyes under his wife's gaze. He began moving his lips as if he were arguing with himself. Surya's wife busied herself with filling the plates. Ram could not help fidgeting in his chair and stealing glances at Surya. It seemed like the argument went on forever. Slowly, Surya started smiling, albeit a thin smile.

"Who will sweep the floor? Who will put the pots and pans outside in the morning? Who would restock the bins? I have got used to you doing these things."

"Maybe Indra could help you for a few hours each day," Ram responded helpfully and hopefully. "He will be off from his studies then, too, and I am sure he would like the change."

Silence. Everyone was eating again, heads concentrating on their plates. The children had washed the sticky food off their hands and gone out to play. Now there were only Surya, his wife, and Ram in the room. The usual clattering of the pots and pans had stopped. All that could be heard was the scrape of fingernails across the plates, the occasional smacking of lips, and the distant shouts of the children outside.

"Maybe," was Surya's slow reply.

Chapter Ten

RAM AND SHYAM'S FIRST GOOD-BYE

Chapter Ten

RAM AND SHYAM'S FIRST GOOD-BYE

It had been six months since Shyam and Karna had left Ram in Bhaktapur. That parting had been difficult for all three of them. Shyam and Ram relived those parting moments in the months that followed. They had been a part of each other's lives since they were born.

"Namaste, Ram," said Shyam as they stood at the front door.

Ram bowed to his father.

"God bless you," said his father.

Ram tried to hide the tear that trickled down his cheek as he bowed deeply to Baa. Ram and his father shook hands in the dim light of the single lamp and then Shyam and Baa headed out the door. Baa was fighting his emotions, too, and spoke in a gruff voice.

"Hurry on. We must get the five o'clock bus to Kathmandu so we can get the bus to Jiri," he said.

Shyam was tired. He and Ram had talked into the night and the floor had been so hard that he hardly slept. It was just as well he was so sleepy. It made the parting less painful. He was going to miss his brother and their long talks. Now he joined his father walking purposefully through Durbar Square. Shyam tried to catch a last glimpse of the wood carvings there, but it was too dark.

Obviously, Baa was anxious to make that first bus to Kathmandu. Then he had to figure out the right bus for Jiri and buy the tickets. Even though they were sad about leaving Ram, they were both wanted to get home and needed to get the earliest and fastest bus. Shyam did not dare to interrupt his father's thoughts. The bus to Kathmandu was crowded already, but Karna and Shyam squeezed on. Karna stepped off the bus almost before it stopped in Kathmandu.

"Shyam, get on that bus over there," Karna said as he turned from the ticket window. "You have seat number 17A. I have 4D," Baa said. As interesting as the city was, even at that early hour, Shyam fell immediately to sleep leaning against the window. The last he heard was the roar of the engine, and the prolonged honk of the bus as it emerged from the parking lot. He managed to get awake enough to get off the bus at the lunch break, and to eat some of the rice, lentils and greens that Baa had bought for him in the teahouse. Otherwise, he slept all the way to Jiri where they spent the night with a friend of Karna's.

"Come on, get up," said Baa as he shook Shyam's shoulder the next morning. "It is almost daylight and I want to get home today."

Shyam was still tired, but he got up quickly, splashed some water on his face, and gratefully accepted the tea from his father's friend. Shyam was anxious to get home, too, to see the rest of the family and get back to work. The two men headed up the trail from Jiri at a fast clip.

Shyam's was looking forward to handling wood and shaping it for doors and windows. They were working on another Gurung house. He would like to talk to Baa about it, but they were walking so fast he could do little more than concentrate on the trail. There wasn't time to talk. The trail was well-worn, and now that he had traveled it once, he had an easier time keeping up with his father.

He started thinking about his mother, Purna, Devi, and Sashi. Sashi was cute now that she was walking. Purna was growing up, too. Shyam would have to get to know him better. Purna was being much more help with the building now, freeing up Shyam to do more cutting and planing. Joints were no longer a problem. His thoughts turned to what he had seen in Bhaktapur. He was eager to develop new designs of his own, based on the sketches he had made.

Then for some reason Shyam started thinking about Tara, a schoolmate in the class behind theirs. Why was he thinking about her? Some nights Ram could do nothing but talk about her when he was home. She was a pretty girl with long black hair and a smooth complexion. She had a beautiful singing voice. He could understand Ram's liking for her. He wondered what Tara thought of Ram. Shyam liked her friendliness. He always felt good talking with her. It made him forget about his shyness.

"We've got just one more hard climb," said Baa, breathlessly. He had stopped briefly to catch his breath and study the rushing river they had just crossed. He was always happy when he got to this point. "It looks like we will get home for a late supper," Baa continued. "I'm hungry. I hope Aama has something for us. We had better keep going."

In spite of their attempts to hurry, the two men moved more slowly in the afternoon, since they were both tired. The hillside was steep, the crevasse moving from one terrace to the next on a bed of rocks. Even though it was still early spring, it was hot when they were moving. They found themselves stopping more and more frequently to wipe their faces and drink from the stream flowing beside them.

As they neared the village, they heard Purna and Devi scampering down the hill, both shouting at once.

"Shyam!"

"Baa!"

"Shyam!"

"Baa!"

"Sashi got another cut on her head." said Devi. "She fell off the step to the porch. I guess I wasn't watching her carefully enough. I thought she could walk better than that. Aama's upset over another cut, but at least she said it wasn't my fault this time. Aama cries every night. She says she misses Ram so much already. Shyam, maybe you can make her smile again. We dug ten potato holes this week and I helped with the digging and the fires." Words tumbled out in a constant stream.

"Come on," said Purna as he bowed to his father. "We're hungry and Aama won't let us eat until you get there."

Shyam fairly ran up the hill, following the more nimble Devi and Purna who had run on to tell their mother of the coming arrival. Shyam bowed to his mother as she came out of the house carrying Sashi. Shyam took Sashi from his mother, doing a short dance around with her. Sashi began to cry and reached toward her mother.

"You can't have forgotten me already," Shyam said. "How did you get that cut on your forehead?" Shyam asked as he stroked it gently. Sashi pointed to the step. Her tears stopped and she snuggled next to Shyam. Aama smiled. Purna and Devi danced around Shyam and then ran to grasp their father's hand as he strode into the courtyard. Maya's smile broadened when she saw her husband. *At least she is happy to see this much of the family*, Shyam thought

"Here, wash your hands," Aama said as she came out of the house carrying a small pitcher. She poured a little water into her husband's outstretched hands and then went over to Shyam.

"Supper is ready," Aama continued. "We'll all eat together tonight—except for Ram." Her voice trailed off. She took Sashi in her arms, and led the way into the house and up the steep steps to the second floor. The smells coming from the fireplace were tantalizing, particularly the vegetable curry. Shyam had missed his mother's cooking. She served everyone a big helping of rice, followed by her delicious dal; no one could fix lentils like his mother could. Curry, potatoes, and fresh-made bread were next. They all dug in with scooping fingers.

"Devi, give everyone some curd and some milk," said Maya. "Also, pour your father a glass of chang. I made it fresh today." Karna liked the homemade brew with his meal.

Shyam was glad to be back at home with his family. He missed Ram already. Even though he respected his brother's decision, he could not understand why Ram had left home. For now, Shyam was happy to be enjoying his mother's cooking and thinking about getting back on the job.

Chapter Eleven

MORNING TEA

Chapter Eleven

MORNING TEA

Shyam loved the early morning. It was family time. His mother was up fixing her wonderful steamy milk tea for the family. It was the one time of day when they were all together. Time to wake up. Time to look at the day, the weather, and at what would be going on. It was a time to pause before the day's activities began. Today was lovely and cool. Shyam sat on the wall in the courtyard with the sun coming over the mountain and warming his back. Sipping the warm tea gave him the energy to start the day.

"We will finish the Gurung house today," said Karna. "We have just one more door frame to do and then we need to clean up after ourselves. The work has gone fast with Shyam's help. It has only been two weeks since we got back from Bhaktapur."

"May I save the scrap wood to try some ideas I have?" Shyam asked. "I liked those carvings in Bhaktapur and would like to see if I can do any."

"Sure, just ask me first," Baa replied. They had to be careful with wood because it was getting harder and harder to find. "Don't you think you should try some drawings first? I would like to see your ideas."

"O.K.," Shyam replied. "I can draw and practice carvings until we get some ideas for a house. I was thinking of porch post tops or a front door frame. I'll show you the sketches I made in Bhaktapur. In the meantime I will store the wood on the corner of our porch."

"I have heard of no other jobs," Baa said. "We will have to try to finish the spring planting before Shyam and I get more work. We will all help Aama today and tomorrow at least to finish up the potato planting. When that is done, Shyam and I will start the plowing for the maize. That field will have to be done twice this year. Shyam, I want you to go up the hill and ask Khem Raj

Karki if we can use his bull sometime in the next week. Then get out the plow and the yoke to see if they need any repairs."

Shyam finished his tea quickly and handed the cup to his mother.

"Purna, come with me while I go talk to Karki," said Shyam. He felt a little less shy if someone were with him. That was O.K. with Purna because he wanted to know how to do these things. The two boys climbed up the three terraces to where Karki was already out plowing with his bull. He waived to Shyam and Purna as they climbed the steep steps to his terrace.

"Namaste!" Shyam said. "Baa asked me to check with you about using the bull sometime this week."

"No problem. I should finish this terrace before noon today. Does he need to borrow the plow, too?"

"No, I think ours is in good repair," Shyam replied.

Shyam and Purna raced each other down the hill.

"I'll help you drag out the plow," Purna said. "It looks like Aama and Baa aren't ready yet to go up to the potato field." Baa joined them and the three carried the plow out to where they could work on it. The long oak pole got heavy sometimes.

"It looks to me like all it needs is a good cleaning," Baa said. "The metal tip needs to be pounded in again so it makes a sharper point to dig into the hard soil. Shyam, you stay and do that, while Purna and I go help your mother."

Shyam leaned the pole against the courtyard wall and took up the wooden mallet. He could feel how strong he had become since last year. The mallet swung easily. He guessed it was because of all the woodworking he had been doing. Last year Ram had helped him get the plow ready. The image of his brother kept coming to him. He missed sharing the work with his brother, but even so he got the job done quickly. Within a few minutes he was finished and went to help his family.

They fell quickly into the routine of digging, building fires, covering them up, and then planting in the holes that had been dug the day before. As Shyam dug, he thought about the carvings. He could hardly wait until evening so he could start the sketches his father had suggested.

Unfortunately, it was too late to sketch by the time they finished the day's work. The house was dark when they got home and his mother needed their one kerosene lamp to start their meal. But Shyam had enjoyed his day in the fields. Field work was not as interesting as wood-working, but he liked doing anything out-of-doors. He could not understand why Ram seemed to be choosing an indoor career, and in polluted Kathmandu at that. Shyam did not think he could live in the city, in spite of the richness of the wood-carvings. There were too many people in the city, and too much noise with the taxi horns, bicycle bells, and motorcycles. Trash in the streets and the wandering cows made filthy surroundings. He was eager to get back to planting tomorrow and looked forward to helping with plowing next week.

About a week later, after morning tea, Shyam and his father went to get the bull from Karki. They had a hard time getting him down the steep hill. The worst part was keeping their own feet out from under the hooves. Shyam was glad Purna and Devi had stayed behind. He and his father would have had to watch out for their feet, too. He decided the bull was glad, as he was to get down to the level field. Together Shyam and Baa managed to get the wooden harness on the bull and hooked up the plow.

They started the plowing at the innermost part of the terrace, just where the wall for the next terrace went up. Most of the time Baa drove the bull all the way across, turned, and came back for the next row. Turning was the hard part. Shyam stood on the end of the plow, to keep it running in the ground. Once in a while, particularly on the straight away, he and his father would trade places. They would plant the maize with the next plowing. There would be even more satisfaction when the first maize shoots came up a few weeks from now. They needed to get the job done, so they could harvest the maize before the monsoon started.

Shyam was tired and he was glad to see his mother and Purna heading across the field with their meal. Devi must have stayed behind to watch Sashi. Baa and Shyam were hungry after their two hours of work. Shyam wondered how his mother was able to cook all that food and carry it across the field still on plates. It was a good thing Purna came along to carry the chang and the two glasses. The two men dug into their plates eagerly. Rice, dal, vegetable curry, curd, ghee, pickles, and some chang to drink. They ate heartily because there was still much work to do and between now and the evening meal there would be just snacks such as fried maize, boiled potatoes, bread, and chang. They hoped to complete half the plowing today so they would have to go get the bull only one more time for the first plowing. The second plowing would not take nearly as long.

Chapter Twelve

BACK TO WOOD-WORKING AT LAST

Chapter Twelve

BACK TO WOOD-WORKING AT LAST

Which one should I do? Shyam wondered out loud. Ever since he had returned from Bhaktapur he had wanted to take the sketches he had made and transcribe them into working drawings. He looked over the wood

he had gathered, carefully looking at sizes and shapes. It was hard to draw a surface picture of where to start. Then, after drawing, how could he get to the finished shape? He was gaining more and more admiration for the ancient carvers of Bhaktapur. This would be no easy task. His father sat on the other side of the fireplace, which was still glowing with embers.

"You need to practice with simple shapes first, like balls, eggs, or pyramids," Baa said. "There are some used exercise books over there. Why don't you try drawing some balls, eggs, and pyramids? Then you could draw a circle, or ellipse, or triangle on a block of wood and try carving."

Shyam brought over the pile of exercise books and started through them one-by-one. He got to the sixth one before there was a blank page. The boys had been taught to be thrifty. He got his pencil from his workbag and began sketching, even shading the surfaces to make them three-dimensional. That turned out to be the easy part.

The next day, when he had free time, he tried to carve from his drawings. He made a game with himself to see how closely he could come to the shape he had drawn on paper. The first ones were crude and lumpy. Sometimes blood stained the wood where he cut himself. Baa and Aama watched their son with satisfaction; he would carry on the family tradition. His brother and sister loved to make up games to play with the pieces. Shyam rushed home every night to practice his new skills.

Once in awhile Tara came by when she was late coming home from school. Shyam guessed she missed Ram, and decided she wanted to at least see his family. She and Shyam had some lively conversations. She seemed interested in his wood carvings. Shyam felt at ease with her and lost his shyness.

One day, after most of the spring planting had been done, M. B. Basnet stopped by to see Baa. Shyam was sitting on the steps working contentedly on his wood carving. He was glad to be there because he could hear everything the men were saying.

"I have just bought a big piece of property just to the West of yours. Do you have time to work on a house for me?" M. B. was one of the more wealthy villagers. He had inherited a lot of land from his father and managed it well. "I want a big house because my two sons are getting married and their wives will live there, too."

This house would be larger than any that Shyam and Baa had worked on before. There were two doors and many windows. M. B. was even talking about having glass brought from Kathmandu for the windows. They would be busy there for a long time.

"When will the masons start?" Baa asked.

"Day after tomorrow," replied M. B. "Today we drove stakes in the ground for the plan and tomorrow they will start digging for the foundation. I am having trouble finding porters to carry in the rock, though."

"You should have the walls far enough along next week that we can see where the windows and doors will be," said Baa. "That will give us time to finish up the spring planting."

"Namaste," said M. B.

"Namaste," said Baa.

The two men shook hands, and M. B. went off in search of porters. A couple of men were hired to carry the rock and the masons were able to start construction on time. Shyam and his father set up their work station out of the way of the masons, but convenient to the house.

In the past year and a half Shyam had improved his skills enough that father and son worked in a rhythm sawing, cutting, planing, and fitting. Shyam and his father worked long hours to try to get the doors and windows framed up as quickly as the masons had finished their work.

M. B. Basnet had ordered the windows from Kathmandu. They would come encased in wood and fit in the frames Shyam and his father made. The carpentry would have to be very accurate so the windows would fit correctly. On the day the porters carried the first windows into the village, Shyam held his breath. Would they fit? Shyam and Baa hoisted the first one into the designated spot. The window was about a centimeter too large. A minor problem. Shyam was able to whittle the frame to accommodate it. Thank goodness the other windows fit with only minor adjustments. The rest of the windows would arrive the next day.

Shyam continued to practice his carving at every opportunity, although Saturday was about the only available time because they were so busy. Soon they would be framing up the porch, putting in support posts and the heavy beams for the roof. Shyam hoped to be able to carve the tops to the four posts at the front of the porch and to make a frame for the main doorway

He got out all of his sketches and, with his father's and Tara's help, he began to choose what he wanted to do. He knew he must keep it simple for this first job. He decided on a plain animal head for the tops of the posts. All four posts would be the same. Then he would try to do an animal for the door frame with the head at the right and the tail at the left. Baa cringed.

"That door frame will be too difficult," he said. "Why don't you do a porch post first and see how it goes?"

Shyam and his father selected a long straight log, and the two men worked it down into the post, leaving a block at the top for the carving. Shyam worked carefully with his carving, rounding the head, and leaving a flat place at the top to go under the porch roof. Tara came by daily now to watch the progress. Shyam was pleased with himself when he was able to carve eyes and ears. The whole family and M. B. watched with anticipation as Shyam and Baa slid the post in place. It worked! By the time Shyam had finished the other three posts he decided his father was right. The whole animal would be too hard.

"Why don't you do a straight lintel with an animal head at each end," suggested his father.

"Maybe I can carve some fur along the lintel," Shyam responded.

And so it was.

M. B. had a big feast at the completion of the house. He even slaughtered a goat. Purna and Devi had fun showing their school friends the animal heads.

"I like the ears and the eyes," exclaimed Purna.

"I like the fur best," said Devi.

Shyam was proud in a way, but he really wanted to show off to Ram. He had thrown himself into his work, but he missed having his twin to help him make the decisions. Just then, Surya's brother, Ramesh, came trudging up the trail. He had just come from Kathmandu. He was hot and dusty, and out-of breath. Before greeting family and friends he splashed water on his face and took a long drink from the new water tap.

"Guess what?" he said. "I stayed with Surya in Bhaktapur while I was in Kathmandu. He said he thought he might let Ram come home for Dashain. It begins in only two weeks."

Chapter Thirteen

WELCOME HOME, RAM!

Chapter Thirteen

WELCOME HOME, RAM!

Purna, take this bamboo tray and get some more marigold blossoms before the sun gets too high, said Aama. "I'm glad we planted all of those seeds last spring."

"I want a garland to give to Ram when he comes," said Devi.

"Me, too," echoed Sashi. She was just beginning to talk, and "Me, too" was her favorite phrase.

"If we all give him one, that will·be six," said Aama. "We'll need to work faster. The messenger said Ram was to leave Kathmandu the day before yesterday. It would take him one day to reach Jiri by bus, then one day of walking here. That means he will be here late this afternoon."

Shyam had not seen his mother so happy in a long time, really since before Ram left. He was glad the whole family was helping to make Ram welcome. Sashi was getting good at tearing flowers from stems, although she ripped off some petals in the process. Never mind. They could throw the petals over Ram's head. Devi was getting better at stringing blossoms, even if she pricked her finger sometimes. Their mother cut thread and threaded needles while the children strung the gay gold and burnt orange blossoms. Shyam was having a hard time containing his excitement. He had missed his brother.

As soon as the garlands were completed, Shyam took the hands of Purna and Devi and pulled them toward the trail.

"Let's go meet Ram," Shyam said.

"Me, too!" said Sashi.

That was the first time Shyam had heard his father really laugh in a long time.

Baa picked up Sashi and hoisted her on his shoulder and they all started down the trail. Aama stayed behind to spread rugs on the porch for her returning son. She had hardly placed the last one when she heard her family's excited voices. She hadn't even started the tea. She ran into the house, filled the kettle with what was left of the water in the jug, and put the kettle on the fire.

"Aama!" Ram shouted as he hurried up the path and bounded across the courtyard toward his mother as she came out the door. He bowed to Aama and then hugged her. He had not hugged her since he was a little boy.

"Sit down, Ram," Aama said as she led him to the edge of the porch. "I was just starting to fix tea."

"Tea?" said Baa as he set Sashi down and joined them. "I think this calls for raksi for Ram and Shyam and me." The family still had saved several bottles of the homemade wine for the Dashain Festival.

"Me, too!" said Sashi. Everyone laughed. Starting with Aama, each person placed a marigold garland over Ram's head. He grinned with pleasure and greeted each one with, "Namaste!" Purna and Devi vied for who could sit closest to Ram. Shyam crouched in front of his brother, just looking up into his face with a smile. They understood each other. They would talk later. Everyone else seemed to be talking at once as they drank tea and raksi.

"Purna, go and fill the jug with water," directed Aama. "Devi, bring out a pan full of water so you can wash the cups and glasses," said Aama.

"This is the first day of Dashain," said Aama. "Today we must sow some of the barley and maize seeds I have saved so they will sprout before Dashain ends. Purna, maybe you could do that this year. While Devi is washing the cups and glasses, you could plant the seeds in the dark corner behind the door. You and Devi can keep them watered every day."

Ram was exhausted from the long climb. He could not wait until dinner was over and he could go to bed. Preparations for Dashain could wait until tomorrow as far as he was concerned.

The next morning Shyam and Ram and their father sat on the wall finishing their morning tea. The sun coming over the mountain shone on the white houses across the valley, but their house was in shadow still and looked dingy by comparison.

"Shyam and Ram, we must paint the house so it will be fresh for the holidays," said Baa. "I got some good white crushed rock. We should get started right away so most of it can dry by nightfall."

"Not until we show Ram the new house," said Shyam. "I have something special to show him."

The boys were glad to have some time alone together as they walked across the terraces to the new house.

"I need some time to talk to you and Baa," Ram began. "I want to start a business on my own in Kathmandu. I see Surya doing things in his business that don't make sense to me. I have so many ideas and he never lets me try anything." Ram was talking very fast now that he had a willing listener.

"Then why don't you come back here and start your own business? We could put up a small building and you could open your own store. We miss you. Aama and Baa need your help." Shyam was warming to his subject.

"I need to finish what I set out to do," Ram interrupted. Then he realized he needed to try a different approach and thought it best to change the subject for now.

"Did you ever do anything with those sketches you made when you were in Surya's house? Have you tried to do any carving? I bet you could get a job helping with the restoration work in Bhaktapur.

"Look at that!" Ram put a hand on Shyam's shoulder. "That is the biggest house you and Baa have ever worked on. Look at all of those windows with glass! You and Baa must work well together, now."

"Come on around to the front. There is more to see," Shyam replied.

"Wow! Did you do those carvings? That's a silly question," Ram said as he answered himself. He reached up with his fingers to feel the eyes and the ears on the heads. "I had to touch them to see if they were real. Now I know you could get a job in Bhaktapur."

"But then, we wouldn't have this house for our village," Shyam said. "I want to make our village a better place to live."

When they came back from the new house, Tara was helping Devi with the dishes, talking companionably. All conversation stopped when Ram and Shyam came down the steps. Tara stood up, looked from one to the other and then cast down her eyes; Shyam and Ram both wondered what caused her to avoid looking at them. She had always been so friendly.

"Hello, Ram," she said timidly.

"Hello, Tara," Ram said a little too heartily. He had been thinking about Tara as he raced up from Jiri. He wondered if she had changed. Ram knew she liked him before he left for Bhaktapur. Did she still? Had she changed? Then he started thinking about Chandra. He liked Chandra and he liked Tara. What was he to do?

Ram thought Tara must have heard that Ram had arrived. Otherwise, why had she come to their house? Then she did a strange thing; she went over and sat beside Shyam.

Chapter Fourteen

ADVICE

Chapter Fourteen

ADVICE

I guess today is paint-the-house day, Ram and Shyam said almost together. The whole family chuckled. Everyone was sitting on the wall of the courtyard looking at the pile of white clay off to the side. Most of the dirt in the area was brown, but there was a seam of almost-white clay over in the next valley. Baa and Shyam, with some porters, had helped carry it back. Sashi toddled over and started picking up fistfuls of clay and letting them drop, giggling to herself.

"I haven't heard you use the same words for a long time," Aama laughed. "You used to do that often when you were little boys. I guess that is because you are twins.

"Not in your mouth," Aama yelled as she picked up the baby, and sat Sashi beside her on the wall, offering her some milk.

"This is paint-the-house day," repeated Baa. "Shyam and I were going to do it ahead of time, but thought we would like you to share the day with us."

"Thanks," said Ram. "Thanks for saving work for me to do," he teased. "I like for us to do things together. We have been separated for a long time, and besides I have some things I want to talk to you about."

"Shyam, you and Purna start carrying water. Ram, you come and help me start with the mixing," Baa directed as he stood up.

"I guess that means it's time to start getting our meal ready," Aama said with a sigh as she set Sashi on the ground. "Devi, go get some water for soaking the lentils and cleaning the rice." Sashi picked up a tea cup that had been left behind and toddled in after her mother. Ram could not take his eyes off his baby sister. She had grown up so much in the six months while he was gone.

Baa picked up the large bucket and handed a stick to Ram. Together they filled the bucket half full of clay. By then Shyam was back with the water and they started mixing. It was hard work at first and Ram and his father passed the stick back and forth. Shyam, found another stick and started loading clay into another smaller bucket.

"I'm thinking of changing jobs," Ram said during one of his rest periods. He had decided to plunge right into his problems. He talked a little about his difficulty getting along with Surya, but more about his thoughts on how Surya ran the business. Ram had developed some ideas of his own.

"Baa, what do you think about me trying a business on my own?"

"I think you should stay where you are..." replied Baa.

"You could start your own hardware business," Shyam interrupted. "Baa and I could show you how to use different tools so you could demonstrate to your customers. I think you should sell only building hardware."

"Shyam, you sound like a business man. You sound like my partner already," replied Ram.

"No way," Shyam replied. "I like what I am doing here too much. I'm just talking about some things I would like to see in a store if I have a chance to go to Kathmandu."

"Can't you use these ideas in Surya's business?" interjected Baa. "It seems to me it is a better idea to work within an established store."

"Surya won't listen," was Ram's simple reply.

By now the men had finished their mixing and were leaning on their sticks as they talked. The sun was climbing in the sky and it was getting hot.

"Purna, go get the brushes we made," Baa said. "You can paint some of the lower parts." They soon developed a rhythm of dipping the brushes and spreading the paint so they could talk again.

"We have no money to help you start a business," said Baa. "There will be rent to pay and you will have to buy supplies. You will have to start out very, very small. You need to be nice to Surya. He has been helpful to you. Surya's been in the business a long time and you ought to listen carefully to his advice."

Ram thought Baa was right about most of these things, but he couldn't figure out how to make it all work Baa's way. *How am I going to make things right with Surya? How can I make money if I start out small? Where else can I get the money?* He had much to think about. Painting was mindless enough that he could think, but his mind was going around in circles.

His thoughts were interrupted as Aama came out of the house carrying a pan full of water to empty, followed by Devi carrying Sashi. Ram quickly finished the part of the wall he was working on and went to join his mother at the side of the courtyard. Shyam, Baa, and Purna finished, too, and joined them. They all admired the freshly painted wall.

"I like it," said Devi.

"When are you going to use the blue paint Ram brought from Bhaktapur for the windows?" Aama asked.

"How did you know what that can was for?" Ram replied. "We need to let the clay dry. We can paint the windows tomorrow. Now I want to go find my old math teacher. He lived in Kathmandu when he was in school and he has had some business experience. I want to get some advice from him, too."

"He's probably up at the school," Shyam said. "Class IX and Class X are having a game of volley ball. Your math teacher is always the scorekeeper. Let's go. I want to watch anyway."

* * *

87

"Namaste," Ram heard from across the field. It was the math teacher. Ram ran over and bowed and they shook hands. Ram and his teacher stood and smiled at each other for a few minutes. "How's the businessman?" asked the teacher.

"I want to talk with you, but don't you have to get the game organized?" Ram asked.

"The English teacher can do that. I am only the scorekeeper. Let's talk."

The two men squatted down off to the side of the field. Shyam joined them. They sat companionably for a few minutes while the teacher smoked a cigarette.

"If you were running a business in Kathmandu, what would it be?" Ram began.

"I think he should open a hardware business," responded the usually taciturn Shyam. "Baa and I know a lot about that, and besides, Ram has been working in Surya's hardware store for six months." Shyam surprised himself, giving Ram all of this encouragement when he really wanted him to stay in the village. He guessed he just wanted to see Ram succeed.

Ram quickly described the business and his problems with Surya.

"I think it is time to go into business for yourself," the teacher agreed.

"Where will I get the money?" answered Ram.

The math teacher considered for a moment, while he lit another cigarette.

"You need to make friends with a banker or someone who is good friends with a banker. You need a bank loan."

"How does a bank loan work?" asked Ram. The teacher described the loan process. The three men went on to discuss different ways of setting up a store. Shyam was excited and got caught up in the plans. He brought up his idea about demonstrating tools. Again, he was lending encouragement for his brother's ventures in Kathmandu. The teacher nodded slowly as they went over all of the ideas.

"Just be sure you maintain a business focus," the teacher said. "Perhaps you want to concentrate on the building trades. Forget about the pots and pans. You want to learn all you can about what goes into building. Then you can give out information." Shyam smiled as the teacher followed along with his own ideas. "Get to know who's building the big buildings, like hotels," continued the teacher. "You need big buyers as well as little people like Surya's customers who buy only a few small things for themselves."

"We need our scorekeeper," someone yelled.

Chapter Fifteen

KNIFE SHARPENING

Chapter Fifteen

KNIFE SHARPENING

Early on the big feast day for Dashain, Ram was alone, sitting on the courtyard wall, sharpening his knife. A goat was tethered to a makeshift open shed to his left.

As he sat, he couldn't help but wonder about his Bhaktapur family and what they were doing. Ram thought they were preparing for an even bigger feast, but he knew he was glad not to be hearing, *It's not worth doing if you can't do it right.* Yet he wondered if in all the years before he went to Bhaktapur, his knife hadn't been sharp enough. He decided to do an extra good sharpening job today, to see if it helped in skinning the goat. Ram surprised himself, in wanting to show his parents he had learned something from Surya after his criticism. A sharp knife was particularly important this time since the family had raised the goat themselves for this special day. His mouth was watering already for the feast they would have.

To sharpen his knife, he needed to go slowly and carefully. Ram had much time to think. He was confused. He had all kinds of different feelings about his life now. What was he to do? Surya had the right idea about doing things correctly, but Surya was abrasive with his criticism. How did he know what was correct? Yet Ram felt Shyam and his father and his math teacher did not understand his difficulties. He was not sure they supported him in the move he wanted to make.

Even though they said it did not matter, he thought that they were unhappy about him working with a Tuladhar, outside the clan's accustomed work. Woodworking is what the family had been doing forever. But why? Farming for food took up most of their time or else they couldn't eat. There was little time for other activities. Why must they be confined to woodworking? Ram enjoyed using his head for figuring and convincing people to buy. Woodworking bored him. He felt he was not using his mind.

Life in the village seemed to have changed since he left. Ram liked the cleaner air and being outside more, but there was not as much to do. He hated to admit it, but the holidays and feast days in Bhaktapur had been fun. It was nice to be speaking Nepali again, although Newari was no longer a threat to him. And then he started thinking about Chandra and how lovely she was and how smart she was. Yet he felt the same old fondness for Tara. Why was she always going to sit by Shyam? He was confused about his own feelings.

Shyam came out of the house carrying his khukuri.

"You started ahead of me on sharpening your knife," Shyam said as he crossed the courtyard. "I think Baa wants us to take care of the goat this year. I'm glad he's giving us more responsibility. We'll need our knives very sharp for skinning the goat, so we can do an extra good job.

"You're lucky to be out on your own, so you can do things without proving yourself," Shyam persisted.

Ram shrugged, "So then why don't you come with me? "We could get a room together and you could help me in the new business."

Shyam sighed. *Ram doesn't understand,* Shyam mused. *Ram has changed. He doesn't seem to care as much about the village anymore. All he thinks about is business in Kathmandu. Even though Baa doesn't give me as much independence as I would like, I love my village and I intend to go on the rest of my life making beautiful things for it. I thought I had made that clear.*

Aloud Shyam said, "I can't leave the village. I have thought it over and I want to spend the rest of my life here. I want to marry and have children, a house of my own, and to continue to make beautiful carvings."

Both boys had tears in their eyes. It seemed inevitable that they would be living apart.

"Here, Shyam, feel my knife."

"Where did you learn to sharpen a knife so well? You never have to sharpen tools all of the time like I do," said Shyam.

Ram had to admit that Surya had worked with him.

"Let me feel yours," said Ram. "Your knife is sharper. I can tell you depend on sharp tools for your daily work." The tears held back and the boys felt their old companionship returning. They continued to sit for a while.

"Shyam, what do you think of Tara?" asked Ram.

"I think she really wanted to see you again. She has come to our house many times since you left. I thought it was because she wanted to be close to your family."

"Then why is she always coming to sit beside you, Shyam?"

"I didn't notice," responded Shyam. "I like talking to her, but I'm not much interested in girls right now."

"Well, she sits by you every chance she gets. You were the one who said he wanted to marry in the village."

"That's some day," responded Shyam.

Now it was Shyam's turn to be confused. He and his brother were always such good friends and now they could not agree on anything. But he still felt the same old fondness for his brother. He was having a hard time admitting that their lives were going in different directions.

"Baa said I could lead the goat around back," Purna said as he came out of the house. "Can I watch the slaughter? I want to watch you skin it, too."

"No," said Ram. "You're too young."

"Yes," said Shyam at the same moment. "You are going to have to learn to help when Ram goes back to Kathmandu."

Shyam and Ram looked at each other in disbelief. This is the first time they had ever given opposing answers.

Chapter Sixteen

THE DASHAIN FEAST

Chapter Sixteen

THE DASHAIN FEAST

Shyam and Ram were smiling again as they became completely involved with slaughtering the goat. They cut off the head and placed it to one side. Then they began the tedious process of removing the fur from the skin.

"Your knife is very sharp. The fur is coming off, leaving a smooth skin," said Shyam.

"Thanks. Yours is doing well, too."

Baa came with a pitcher of water to pour over the goat. The twins methodically cut the goat into pieces and placed them in a large tub. Later the women would cut them to bite-size. Ram and Shyam extracted the intestines, pouring water through the tubes to clean them.

"The organ meats are my favorite parts," Shyam said. "I hope they cook these up quickly so we can eat them as a snack."

"Me, too," said Ram. "I am hungry already."

"Me, too," said Sashi.

"Where did she come from," Ram and Shyam said together.

At least they could agree on the little things, Shyam thought. He picked up Sashi and carried her around the house where the women were getting ready to cook.

"Come," Aama said. "You are just in time. We are going inside to the worship place to make our offerings to the gods. All seven Newar families in the village are here, so you boys must stand at the back."

As they crowded into the house, Ram noticed Tara was there, right up front next to the small worship place sculpted into the wall. He noticed the carving had been redone. Some of Shyam's work, he guessed. Tara lit the oil lamp on the small shelf. One member from each family squeezed forward to make an offering. Ram felt Tara was the most graceful in her movements as she made her offering of marigolds and the yellow seedlings they had planted at the beginning of Dashain. Ram realized how beautiful she had become. He was surprised at how agitated he became as Tara looked up with a sparkle in her eye, right at Shyam. Just then he felt someone shoving him. It was Sashi toddling through the crowd with her fists clenched tight.

"Me, too," she said as she threw marigold petals at the worship place.

Slowly everyone filed outside.

The smells became increasingly tantalizing as the women added more spices to the cooking goat. Karna stirred the rice. It took a big pot to feed so many people. Tara and some of the other girls finished preparing vegetables to cook with the rice. Tara shelled peas, while other girls cut up walnuts, dates, and coconut.

Shyam and Ram sat silently under the apple tree at one side. They were still upset over their differences. They seemed unapproachable. Karna and Maya exchanged questioning looks as they noticed the boys' glum faces and their silence. Ram got up quickly, picked up a handful of pea pods and sat beside Tara.

"I'm glad your family came today," Ram said as he started to shell his peas. "I like it when all of the Newars get together. When I am in Bhaktapur, I live with Newars, only it is different. I have had to learn some of the Newari language. There are lots of Newar families there and they have many festivals. It would be nice if you could to Kathmandu and Bhaktapur someday." Tara looked at her friends and smirked. Ram didn't know what the smirk was all about. "Maybe after dinner we can go watch the games and dancing up at the playground," he finished lamely.

"We're ready for the vegetables," Maya shouted. She had just put some oil and spices in a large pan, stirring them quickly as the girls brought what they had cut up. The fire was just right for slowly frying them with the spices. When the vegetables were soft, Karna added some of the rice to make fried rice. That meant dinner was almost ready. Ram got up and went back to sit by Shyam.

"I'm ready to eat," said Shyam.

"Me, too. It's been a long wait," said Ram. He was trying hard to force a smile, desperately trying to remain friends with his brother in spite of their differences.

"What were you and Tara talking about?" asked Shyam. He wanted to be friends, too.

Ram was silent for a moment. He had to be honest with his brother.

"I was telling her about the Newars in Bhaktapur," Ram replied.

"Here are your plates," Devi said as she danced by. "Aama says to get in line."

"We're ready," Ram and Shyam said in unison. They were both smiling as they got to their feet.

"We'll talk more later," said Shyam as he picked up his leaf plate to go and get in line.

Ram and Shyam took both the steamed rice and the fried rice, goat meat, cauliflower, and dal. Shyam hoped his brother's temper would improve with the food. He couldn't understand Ram's love of the city. Now, he was trying to get Tara interested. He shook his head and went to sit by Ram. By then the girls were getting their food. Tara came over to sit by Shyam.

"Do you have to leave tomorrow?" Shyam asked.

"Yes, I promised Surya I would leave the next day after Dashain. Why can't you come with me for a few days?"

"I can't. Baa and I are still working on that house. You might say I have a job, too," Shyam said tersely. "Are you going to tell Surya about your new plans?"

"I want to do that right away. I want to become established as soon as possible."

Tara watched both boys with questioning eyes. *Why is Ram telling me about Bhaktapur? Doesn't he notice I am not interested?*

Shyam looked at Tara. *Does she still like Ram? Is she really showing more interest in me? She is sitting with me more.* He glanced over at her. She looked sadder now. *Is it because Ram is leaving tomorrow? Which twin does she like the best?*

Chapter Seventeen

IF YOU CAN'T DO IT RIGHT

Chapter Seventeen

IF YOU CAN'T DO IT RIGHT...

He's here! Ram's back! came the shouts as Ram entered the square. They were talking in Newari, but Ram understood even after his time in the village. It was getting dark with the shortening November days, but he could still make out the faces of the neighbors. In some ways he felt as if he were coming home. Chandra sat on the steps to her house across the square. Yes, she was just like he remembered her. She put her palms together, bowed, and then waved. Indra, sitting on the step above, waved, too. Ram smiled as he pushed through the crowd of children toward Surya's house.

"Namaste! Ram," said Surya's wife as she came down the steps with a marigold garland. He bowed to her and then stooped so she could put the garland over his head. It was good to be back again.

Ram took his shoes off at the doorway, put them to one side, and started into the living room. There was Surya sitting on the couch, his arms folded, and a frown on his face. Ram's smile faded quickly.

"What took you so long?" growled Surya. "Indra went back to school two days ago. I have had to do all the work myself. I told you to be back here right after Dashain."

Ram stared in disbelief. He knew, though, that it would do no good to say that his family had their feast the day before yesterday and it took two days to get to Bhaktapur.

"I am sorry it took two days to get here. How's business been?" Ram could think of nothing else to say. The good feelings about his welcome evaporated.

"Business will be fine when I can get you back on the job. We better leave a half hour early tomorrow so we can get caught up. Both the nails and screws need restocking, the pots and pans are out of order, and we have had more than the usual number of customers now that Dashain is over."

The next morning Surya began with, "You have put the pans on the wrong side of the door. Pile them only five deep so they don't go clattering to the floor like they usually do. *If you can't do it right, it's not worth doing.*"

If you can't do it right, it's not worth doing. Ram felt the old tension rising. *Why didn't I speak with Surya about my new plans on our way to work?* he said to himself. *Now Surya is cross again. This would not be a good time to bring it up. It would be better to wait until we are on our way home.* Ram had to restrain himself from kicking the pans out into the street. He picked them up and moved them to the other side of the door. He couldn't resist dropping one. He closed his ears to the inevitable, *"If you can't do it right, it's not worth doing,"* but Surya just shrugged and shook his head.

The rest of the day went all right. Nothing had been rearranged since he left. He had hoped that Indra would be able to bring about some changes. Indra's mind was probably on Dashain, and he, too, was a little afraid of Surya's temper. Surya spent most of the day talking to Newar customers who came into the store. He left Ram to restock the bins. Ram was glad not to have Surya looking over his shoulder. Ram had plenty of time to figure out how to approach Surya as he completed this almost mindless task.

"Let's sweep up and put the pots and pans away," said Surya.

All day Ram had been waiting for that time. Now that it was here, his determination was collapsing. He was so nervous, he made more bumbles than usual as he prepared for closing. There was only one "If you can't so it right..." from Surya. At last Ram pulled the metal gate down and pushed the bolt. Surya padlocked the bolt and pocketed the key. They turned toward home.

"I did a lot of thinking while I was on the trail this week." Ram tried to keep his voice even. "You have taught me so much, that I think I could manage a hardware business on my own," Ram said. He was expecting a big explosion at any moment, but when none came, he continued on.

"I talked to my father and my brother and my math teacher. My brother thinks I should concentrate on hardware for the building trades. Baa wants me to be sure and ask you what to do and follow your advice because you have been in business so long." Ram stole a glance at Surya. Surya opened his mouth as if to say something and then closed it again. He did this two or three times. Ram searched his mind trying to think of something else to say, but he just had to have some reaction from Surya first. Surya stopped to greet a friend and then began to mouth his words silently. A few minutes later he started to mutter, but was staring straight ahead, oblivious to Ram.

"How long has he been thinking about this? Who's going to do the work now? I've gotten used to his bumbling ways. He'll be in competition with me. He doesn't know the first thing about running a business. He'll fail and then my brother in the village will be mad at me. But I guess Ram and I don't get along too well. He doesn't understand *If you can't do it right it isn't worth doing.* He does not know how to do it right. I think I will be glad when I don't have to struggle with him anymore." Surya had no idea he was talking loud enough for Ram to hear. He stopped and turned to face Ram.

"Where are you planning to establish this business?"

"I'm thinking about Kathmandu. I always wanted to own a business in Kathmandu." Ram responded.

"Good. Then we won't be in competition," said Surya.

By now they were coming into the square where they lived. As if by agreement both men stopped talking. Surya went in search of his children and Ram went to sit on the steps by Chandra. She had a shawl wrapped around her against the cool evening. It was November now. He gave an involuntary shiver.

"How was Dashain?" Ram asked.

"It was wonderful. All our relatives came and we had two goats. We talked and talked and talked." Ram couldn't take his eyes off her. She was even more beautiful then he remembered. Then he thought of Tara. He sighed. *How could I be so taken with two women? How would Tara get along with the Newars in Kathmandu? Would she be able to learn the language? She goes to school and she should be able to study. Would she like the kind of life people lived here? Tara was a friendly person. She could get along with anyone.* Chandra interrupted his reveries.

"How was your Dashain?" she asked. But before he could answer, she said, "Tihar is in a few days. Why didn't you stay in the village until after it was over? Now you will miss Brother's Day. Never mind. I'll give you tika."

Unlike Tara, Chandra was a chatterer, but he would be thrilled to have tika from her.

Yes. It would have been nice to stay in the village and receive the red dot on his forehead with Shyam. They knew all about Tihar in the village. It was the festival of light, lighting the way to the door for Laxmi, the goddess of wealth.

His family celebrated the five day holiday, too, There was the Day of the Crow, the Day of the Dog, the Day of the Cow, Mha Pujaa, the Newar New Year, and finally, Brother's Day. That is when Chandra would give him tika.

Chapter Eighteen

THE DAY OF THE CROW

Chapter Eighteen

THE DAY OF THE CROW

A few days later Ram awoke and stretched luxuriantly under his cotton quilt. Daylight was beginning to show at the window. He could hear Surya's wife treading heavily down the steps. Soon he would have to get up and carry more wood for the fires. The gas was not working, and the servant was too old to carry the wood into the house. He lay there for a few minutes to think about the day ahead. Tihar began that day.

He reviewed the different days they would be celebrating. Today was the crow's day. The crow got extra seed on his day because he was so smart. Tomorrow would honor the dog because he is so helpful. The following day the cow would wear a marigold garland because she gives milk, and then the Mha Puja, body worship day, followed by New Year's Day for Newars, and finally Brother's Day. Non-Newars celebrate the Day of the Ox, honored for his hard work. In past years, he and Shyam would make garlands for the dog and the cow.

Ram thought with anticipation about the tika he would receive from Chandra on Brother's Day. On this day sisters honored their brothers by giving tika, and the brother usually gave a gift to his sister. He hoped he had a few rupees left from his trip to give Chandra. Brother's Day was always something special for him, but it would be more so this year with Chandra giving him tika.

Ram loved the story behind Brother's Day. The God of Death was coming after a young woman's brother. The woman delayed her brother's leaving by dribbling oil in a circle around him. The sister told the God that her brother could not leave until the oil dried. That way she saved her brother's life. Now sisters honor each brother, decorating his forehead with a fancy tika design of many colors and then dripping water around him three times. Use of incense and marigold petals make the ceremony special. It was the one time of the year girls could show appreciation for their brothers, and brothers could demonstrate respect for their sisters.

"We need some wood and help with the fire," Surya's wife shouted. Ram got up quickly and raced down the stairs to the kitchen. The helper had already stirred the embers and added some corn cobs. Ram brought wood from outside and got the fire going.

"I will be glad when they fix the gas stove," the helper said. The pot boiled quickly and she poured tea for all. Next, she scrambled eggs and mixed in spices and chiura, the beaten rice they all loved so well.

"Can I have some seeds to feed the crows?" asked Surya's daughter. Her mother handed her a few grains of corn from a basket over by the wall. Then, of course, her brother had to have some, too.

"Come on," said Surya, "We must open the store. Customers will not be thinking about crows."

Surya and Ram headed out the door. It was cold, so the two men walked briskly. Ram wished they would slow down, so they could talk more about future plans. Surya had said almost nothing about them in the past week. Ram noticed that lately Surya disappeared at different times during the day, leaving Ram to manage by himself. *Was this a test?* Ram wondered. When he was in the store, Surya would go off in a corner behind the lanterns with one young man or another to have a private conversation.

That morning when they got to the store there was an old man leaning on a stick already waiting. Surya took the key out of his pocket to unlock the padlock and Ram raised the metal gate.

"Ram, go get three cups of tea...and hurry. We don't want to keep Mr. Tuladhar waiting," said Surya.

When Ram got back, Surya started right in.

"Mr. Tuladhar is having some health problems and cannot work in his store in Kathmandu anymore. He has a big place and employs three people who work very hard. He can no longer do the managing on a daily basis. He feels he needs a younger man to operate the business."

Ram could not believe his ears. *Were they talking about him?*

"How much experience have you had?" asked Mr. Tuladhar, looking straight at Ram.

"Well, I have helped Surya for the past six months and before that I was co-manager of a stall at our weekly market in our village," Ram replied. "Now I want to work on my own."

"What kind of work do you want to do?" asked the old man.

"I was thinking of a store specializing in the building trades. My brother and father are carpenters and they think this would be a good business."

"Hardware restricted to the building trades? Sounds like a good idea. A lot of what we sell has to do with building. There is a lot of building going on in Kathmandu right now. But it sounds like you need some training in management. You have never had anyone work for you before and I'm sure Surya has not taught you where and how to get supplies."

Ram's spirits faltered. He wanted to start out fresh with a new business, but he had to admit he had some learning to do. At least Surya had not brought up his problem with *If you can't do it right, don't do it at all.*

"You work with me for nothing for a while, and if all goes well, you can buy me out. I want to leave the business completely. I can even help you with a bank loan."

Ram's surprise was complete. It was hard to believe that Surya had made so much effort on his part. *Why? Had this Mr. Tuladhar approached Surya? Or was Surya trying to get rid of me?*

The three men sipped their tea for a while.

"You can't leave here until I find somebody to replace you," said Surya. "Maybe after Tihar"

Ram wondered, *What other roadblocks will Surya put in front of me?* But Ram was still sure he could make everything work out. Inwardly he was so excited, he wanted to jump up and down and run tell Chandra right away. But he composed himself, only smiling, as he gathered up the tea cups and placed them in the rack on the counter. The three men shook hands and bowed to each other.

The old man shuffled slowly out the door.

Now Ram could enjoy the rest of Tihar.

Chapter Nineteen

BROTHER'S DAY

Chapter Nineteen

BROTHER'S DAY

Ram thought Brother's Day would never come. The Newar New Year came the day before. Ram sensed that he would not be welcome at that family occasion and spent the evening wandering Bhaktapur, watching the people. Children running around. Couples jostling good-naturedly at the temporary stalls. He welcomed the good wishes he got as he purchased some tidbits of food. He thought this much more interesting than subjecting himself to Surya and his family. Besides, he could daydream more about receiving tika from Chandra the next day.

In the morning, almost before Ram finished his tea, Surya was off to visit his two sisters to get his tika. Before he left, he gave Ram the key to the store.

"I will be there in a little while. This will give us a chance to see how well you can manage on your own," Surya said.

After he left, his wife said, "My brother will not be here until later in the day, probably after the store closes. That will give me plenty of time to prepare a special meal, gather some marigold petals, and mix the different colors for the tika. Do you want me to do tika for you, Ram?"

"Thank you for the offer, but I will get my tika from Chandra," replied Ram.

Surya's wife raised her eyebrow, but said nothing.

Ram took his tea glass to be washed, gathered up some tidbits for lunch, and started out the door.

"You had better put on your vest. It's cooler this morning," Surya's wife said.

Ram slipped on his vest, picked up his shoes at the door, and went out. He looked up at the blue sky and smiled. It was cool, but it was clear. He liked this time of year. The monsoon had settled the dust and cleansed the atmosphere. The ornate carvings on the Newar houses rising beside him stood out more clearly now. Today was going to be a good day for him. He kept fingering the key in his pocket. He knew he would do everything right today. The *If you can't do it rights.* came less often now. When he got to the store, he unlocked the padlock and raised the gate. He took three deep breaths before he turned on the lights and started carrying out the pots and pans.

Ram was startled. He was stooping to stock the bins when he noticed a tall, thin, young man standing over him.

"Hello, I am Gopal. I am looking for Surya Tuladhar. My father sent me to see him about a job."

Ram straightened up and put out his hand to Gopal.

"Namaste! My name is Ram. I work for Surya. He will be here in a few minutes. There's a chair over there."

"No, thanks," said Gopal. "I think I will look around." He walked to the back of the store until he ran into so many boxes blocking his way that he had to turn around and came back.

"Do you like working here?" Gopal asked.

Ram hesitated. He did not quite know how to answer.

"It is O.K., but I am wanting to go into business for myself," he replied.

"Namaste!" Surya said as he rushed into the store. His forehead was covered with tika.

"You're Gopal?" Surya asked

Gopal bowed. "Namaste!" he said.

"Ram, go get some tea. Hurry, because I want you to hear what we have to say."

Ram returned in a few minutes, but came around the corner of the store too fast and spilled some tea. Surya looked at him sternly, but kept quiet. Instead, he turned to Gopal.

"Your father says you have been helping him in his clothing store, mostly waiting on customers and collecting the sale price."

"Yes," replied Gopal. "I think I would like a job that is a little more active now and I want to save money to take some business courses."

"Your father doesn't pay you?" asked Surya.

"No, he doesn't have the money."

"Ram, tell Gopal what you do in a day around here," said Surya

"Well, I put out the pots and pans in the mornings, restock the bins, go get tea, sweep the floor, sometimes wait on customers, and keep the store neat and tidy. Surya is very particular," Ram couldn't help adding.

"I really want this job," said Gopal.

Surya put out his hand and they shook hands.

"Report here one week from today. You can work one week with Ram. Then I will expect you to work on your own."

Ram gathered up the teacups, gave a wave to Gopal, and went back to restocking the bins. It was turning out to be a good day as he had thought; now there was nothing standing in the way of his new job and he still had his tika ceremony to look forward to.

The commotion in the street increased as the afternoon wore on. Because of the three and four story buildings, the sun didn't get down to Surya's shop until afternoon. The sun had warmed the air, and its brightness made the day more festive. Everyone seemed to be hurrying somewhere, either to receive tika or to take part in the accompanying festivities.

"You can go now," said Surya. "I have already got my tika. I'll close up. My wife will be ready to give you tika soon."

Ram decided not to say anything. Maybe he could get tika two times. He bowed to Surya and hurried home. He wanted to put on a clean shirt and a topi before going to Chandra's house.

* * *

"Sit over there," directed Chandra.

Should he sit back, so she would have to lean over to give him tika, or should he sit on the edge of the seat so she wouldn't have to reach so far?

"Sit down!" said Chandra.

He tried to act nonchalant as he pushed back a little from the edge of the chair. Chandra picked up the tray of tika material and a small stick. She mixed a little water with each color. Ram closed his eyes as she leaned over to draw the design on his forehead with a stick. He wished it was the other kind of tika, so she would touch his forehead with her finger. The smell from the incense seemed to envelop her. What pleasure he got from this simple ceremony! But, he did not feel like this when his mother gave him tika. In turn he added a line to Chandra's tika, brushing her forehead with his little finger as he did. Chandra's mother thrust a glass of raksi into his hand and then a tray of food. The spell was broken.

Chapter Twenty

AFTER A WHILE

Chapter Twenty

AFTER A WHILE

Ram thought the week with Gopal would never end. He was ready for his new job. Gopal learned quickly. He waited until Ram explained what to do before beginning a task. As a result, he did not bumble the way Ram had. Ram looked back at his own beginnings and wondered why Surya was so upset with him. He guessed part of it was just Surya, and he guessed he had been too impatient to listen when he started something new. Ram was always in a hurry to get to the next thing. But then Surya had little patience himself, and he was a perfectionist. Surya insisted on showing Gopal the cash register part of the job himself. Otherwise, he left the boys alone and spent his days that week talking to his Newar friends. At least that made Ram feel he was doing a good job with the training.

The week did end. Ram spent Sunday washing his clothes, taking a bath, and getting Surya's wife to cut his hair. Even though it would take a long time to get to his new job in Kathmandu every day, he was glad Surya was allowing him to stay there for a while. At least he would not have to worry about feeding himself and he would be able to see Chandra sometimes.

His new boss greeted him warmly and introduced him to the other workers. After tea, his boss showed him how to open and close the store. Ram was pleased with his new responsibility. Surya had not allowed him to open and close until near the end of his employment. Of course, opening and closing everyday meant that he had to come early and stay late, leaving little time with Chandra.

The whole atmosphere was warm and friendly. The first months flew by. He needed to spend much time learning the business. Ram had to learn about how each department was run, and what the responsibilities were for its manager. In addition he had to familiarize himself with the merchandise. One section of the store sold things used in homes, such as kitchen utensils, pots and pans, cups and plates, and eating implements. He had never seen many of the tools, such as a potato peeler or a cheese grater. Ram spent his spare time learning how they worked. *Wouldn't my mother like to have some of these things! Life in the village would be so much easier for her.*

"How do you get more merchandise?" Ram asked.

"Well, we keep track of how much we sell, and then we tell the boss when we are low. He orders more."

That's what he and the math teacher had started doing at the Saturday Market. He was going to have to find out more about how the inventory worked. Maybe he would be able to share some new ideas with his math teacher. After all, it was the math teacher who had been so helpful in getting Ram interested in business.

Another part of the store, up to the right of the front door, had to do with farming. The adzes and plows and other tools took up a lot of space. The few farmers who came in wanted to try them out, but there was no room. Ram thought most of the farmers made their own tools, as his father did. Besides, if they bought tools, how would they ever get them home? Then there were the seeds, right by the door. So many kinds of rice and other grains in sacks. Packets of vegetable seeds filled a long rack. Ram would like to take some of those back to his mother. These were different kinds of seeds than she was accustomed to.

"Where do the seeds come from?" Ram asked the manager.

"We have farmers who bring them in," the manager replied.

"My mother spends a lot of time collecting our seed. It would be nice for her to have more varieties."

The building trades that Shyam was so interested in were in the back of the store. The managers told him that products for the home and the seeds would attract people to the store, like the pots and pans Surya had him put outside every morning. If a customer was interested in the building trades, he came to that store for that purpose, and went directly to the back of the store. Glass, galvanized steel, nails, screws, brackets, and tools were jammed together.

"When people buy glass, how do they get it home?" Ram asked.

"There's a shop down the street that builds frames exactly to the right size. Porters carry them up into the mountains what way," the worker replied.

"I remember now," Ram said. "When my brother and father made windows for the Gurung house in the village, the glass came from Kathmandu. Doesn't it break?"

"Occasionally, but most of the windows get through."

"I have seen porters carrying galvanized roofing sheet, too," Ram continued. "Some of those sheets were two or three meters long. We had to get off the trail to let them pass. The sun shining on them was so bright, I could hardly see."

"The boss is working on having the galvanized and glass shipped to other towns by truck so they don't have to be carried so far," replied the worker.

"But there are no roads to many places," added Ram.

The three managers knew their stock well. Ram bought a small notebook and took lots of notes, jotting down what he saw, what they said, and his new ideas as they came to him.

His new boss had him sweeping the floor and helping the others day after day. That gave him time to study the store and take notes, but there seemed to be no chance for him to implement his new ideas. Ram had many thoughts about methods to restock and about arranging different departments. When he approached his boss, he was met with a smile and good cheer. But the answer was always the same,

"After a while." It was as if the boss was not even listening.

Ram became impatient and bored. He wished that Shyam were there to help him push for the building trades. Ram was running out of ideas about how to approach his new boss. His father and math teacher would have been able to make his thoughts clearer. He could not think of a way to get around the consistent *after a while*, although *after a while* was better than, *If you can't do it right.*

His bus ride back and forth each day allowed him time to think. Ram was bored with the business and was unable to see Chandra because of his long hours. He started thinking about Tara again. If he could marry her, they could get their own apartment close by the store. It was time for him to get away from Surya's anyway. *How would she fit in?* He wondered again about the language problem and how she would adjust to the big city. How could he find out?

Chapter Twenty-One

A BIG SURPRISE

Chapter Twenty-One

A BIG SURPRISE

"Ram! Ram!" exclaimed Surya's son as he raced across the square. Ram was tired. It was Saturday and the store had been particularly busy, but he couldn't help smiling at the boy.

"Guess what? Uncle just arrived from the village," the boy said excitedly.

"And he brought our cousin with him," his sister joined in as she caught up with her brother.

Ram's heart skipped a beat. *Could that mean that Tara came, too?*

"They came for the *Guthi*," the two children continued, but Ram wasn't even listening. He had to find out if Tara had come. He walked quickly across the square and bounded the steps two at a time. He almost forgot to take off his shoes.

Surya's brother stood in the doorway, and gave Ram a warm greeting.

"Namaste!" said Ram. As he bowed, he kept trying to glance around Surya's brother to see if he could see Tara. They shook hands, and then Ram brushed past. There she was, sitting on the couch.

"Namaste, Ram," she said.

"Namaste, Tara. I'm so happy to see you," Ram said. There were many people around, but he found a space to sit at her feet. He was surprised to see that Tara seemed about to cry. *Wasn't she happy to see him?*

"Why don't they talk like we do?" Tara asked, almost sobbing. "I can't understand anything they are saying and I don't understand why these people are here. It isn't a holiday. I just wanted to see you and Auntie and Uncle."

"They are speaking Newari. It's our language. You remember I said something about that when I was home at Dashain. We don't talk Newari in our village because there are so few Newars," Ram explained. "You will learn quickly."

Tara was inconsolable. "The only people I will be able to talk with will be you and my baa. You will be at work each day and I'll just be sitting here on this couch, doing nothing," she sniffled.

"How was your trip?" Ram asked in an effort to change the subject.

"It was nice walking to Jiri. The sun is beginning to warm again now that spring is coming. It's still cool in the village. We haven't started potato planting yet. It got warmer and greener as we headed down the hills. The wheat was showing green and the mustard yellow. Here, in the Kathmandu Valley, it is even greener. I love spring."

Ram's ruse worked for a little while, but then her face clouded up again. "Baa said we were coming to a *Guthi*. I keep hearing that word among all of this talk. What is a *Guthi* anyway? I never heard of it before."

Ram took a deep breath. "We don't have *Guthi* in our village because there are not enough Newars. Your auntie has been preparing for this for weeks. It is her turn this year. There are going to be more than forty people here. I don't know much about it either. We can learn together. Chandra told me that..."

"Who is Chandra?" Tara interrupted.

"She lives across the square," Ram answered quickly and then continued, "Chandra told me the *Guthi* is made up of a tribal group of Newars. The *Guthi* makes the necessary arrangements at the time of a death. At the funeral, just like in our village, the body is covered in a gold body shroud. After the funeral, the shroud is given to the member who is taking charge for that year. Keeping the shroud means the God is living in their home. The *Guthi* meets once a year. From watching your auntie, there will be lots of feasting. Every night when we come home, she has us try another dish. Surya has been taking care of notifying everyone. I think that is why you are here."

"Baa never said anything about it," Tara said.

Over the next days, Tara told Ram that she tried to make friends with others, but she couldn't because she was confronted constantly with a language she could neither understand nor speak. She seemed unable to learn the strange tongue.

"Ram, you are wrong. I will never learn it," she said over and over again.

At first Ram was just as glad because that meant Tara would spend more time with him when he was at home. The only problem was, what was he going to do about Chandra?

"Shyam's letting his hair grow," Tara said one day. "I think it will look nice when it gets long. His face will look thinner that way."

On another day, she said, "Shyam has started on another house. I am helping him decide what carvings to make."

At first Ram was content to sit and listen to her talk. He was delighted to have news about his brother. But Tara talked about Shyam all of the time. She showed no interest in Ram's work. When he came home in the evening, she complained over and over again about the Newari language, and yet refused to try to learn any of it.

On the following Sunday he saw Chandra on her front steps. It was a warm day and he went to sit with her.

"Why are you spending so much time away from home?" Chandra began. "You spend more time working now than you did at Surya's store."

"I think it is a good business opportunity," Ram replied eagerly. "Some day it will be my business and I can fix things the way they ought to be. I have lots of ideas. You should come and see it one day and I can show you everything."

Chandra shrugged. She felt isolated from Ram. He was no longer the country boy she could help.

Ram had an idea. Neither Tara nor Chandra was excited about his job. He decided he would ask Tara's father to bring her to the store the next day, and then, later that week, Indra could bring Chandra. Tara had to visit first because she and her father would be returning to the village. Ram could not stand the strain of having both girls at the store at once. He was eager to have them like what he was doing. Part of his vision was to make it a family business. He was disappointed in them both for their lack of warmth for his proposed career.

Ram was not very well pleased with the results of his little scheme. Tara seemed overwhelmed by the visit. She had not been inside any stores other than a few small shops in Bhaktapur. Although her interests were in the household items, the farm implements, and the building materials Shyam might use, the size of the place was too much.

"Are you going to be a manager of all this?" she asked. "How can you do it by yourself? This is too big."

"Here, look at this," said Ram. "This will grate cheese or carrots." Ram demonstrated with his hand. "Would you like one? Do you think you could take one to my mother when you go back to the village?"

"I can take one for your mother, but I like doing things the old way." Ram was not getting very far. Tara said, "I know your father and Shyam will be proud of you if you succeed in a business, but this store is too big. You can't find anything."

But she didn't say anything about being proud herself and she found so many faults with the store. I wonder if she could be part of the picture, Ram reflected.

Chandra's visit was different. She was more accustomed to big stores. She was interested in seeing what he did, but at the same time maintained an annoying indifference, Ram thought.

"This is a big store," said Chandra. "It looks like it would be a lot to manage, but I am sure you can do it. I'm not much interested in farms or building materials. I want to keep a nice house when I marry, but I don't think it requires all this stuff," she said. She swung her arm across the building materials, the farm equipment, and the agricultural department. "Perhaps you can do only one section of it. I know you will have a successful business no matter what part of it you do. Anything will be possible for you."

Ram was back at the beginning. He was silent as he and Chandra and Indra caught the bus to Bhaktapur. He shivered. It was cool without the sun. Tara liked what he was doing, but lacked the confidence that he would be successful. Chandra did not like the type of business, but thought Ram would be a good business man. What was Ram to do?

Chapter Twenty-Two

THE OLD MAN

Chapter Twenty-Two

THE OLD MAN

Spring came, quickly followed by the monsoon. It rained almost every day. Frequent thunderstorms punctuated the afternoons. Planting time had come and gone. In spite of signs outside the store, the farm section might as well have not been there. The farmers stayed away. Their agriculture equipment was not selling. Only the seeds. Ram decided to approach his boss again.

"Namaste," Ram said as he bowed deeply. "May I talk to you a minute?"

"Of course."

Ram laid down his notes as he slid into a chair next to his boss.

"I would like to propose that we get rid of the agriculture equipment," Ram said. "Here are the figures for the past four months."

The boss spent some time studying the neat columns.

"I can't argue with these figures," his boss said. "What do you suggest?"

"Well, why not have a sale? How much did you pay for these plows? Can we sell them at cost? What about putting some sign boards on the way into Kathmandu?"

"One question at a time, please. You do have some ideas. We'll talk to the other managers."

All of them embraced the idea except for the manager of the farm department who was afraid he might lose his job.

"We'll keep the seeds," said Ram. "With more of us to work at it, we'll be able to push the other merchandise harder." He hoped he had reassured the manager. Besides, another of his plans was to change the seed section to sell flower seeds and potted plants having to do more with buildings.

"I'll support this," replied the boss. He appointed the farm equipment manager to take charge of the project with Ram's help.

Ram was elated. At last they were on the way to making their business more specific. They put large signs outside the store and then on the ring road around Kathmandu. Few farmers came for a while, but then they began to trickle in. Ram even tried to arrange transportation for them. Gradually, that area of the store began to clear out and they could move other merchandise so the aisles were not so crowded. The weather continued to be steamy, hot and rainy. Ram was exhausted from helping the farmers load wagons, trucks, taxis, and rickshaws.

He noticed his boss had more and more problems getting around. The boss walked with two canes and Ram had to help him in and out of his car every day. Ram wondered how long it would be before his boss would not be able to come to work at all. Ram felt badly, but, at the same time, he was ready to make the business his.

There was another problem. He wanted to go home for Dashain, to see Tara, and to talk to Shyam, his father, and his math teacher about the business again.

As if these problems were not enough, Surya was saying that Ram would have to move out of the house soon. Ram thought the request was reasonable, but he did not know where to go. After a particularly trying day at the store, Surya said,

"I think it is time you got out on your own. You are from a different family. My children are growing older and I am going to have to think about their needs. If you marry, you can find an apartment close to your store. What would your parents think if I acted as go-between to look for a bride for you? They don't know the eligible women in Kathmandu."

Ram was puzzled. All along he had been hoping the choice would be his. *Otherwise, why was he working so hard to make up his mind between Chandra and Tara?*

"Will I have any choice?" Ram asked.

"Of course. Is your boss going to let you go home for Dashain? You could take pictures with you and describe the choices to your parents then."

Would Surya even consider Chandra? he wondered.

No more was said. Now Ram was going to have to figure out how to get away for Dashain with his boss so dependent on him. That was the all-important yearly festival when everyone visited family. Fortunately, the boss was late the next morning and the managers were there early. They agreed he could go home for the first week of Dashain if he would come back to let them off for part of the second week. Ram would miss the feast with his family, but that would have to be.

His boss was really late that morning. It took two of them to get him out of the car. He was not even driving anymore.

"I want to meet with you while there are no customers here," he said to Ram. He sat down heavily at his desk, and put his head in his hands. The managers tried to look busy in their departments. The boss was quiet for a few moments. Eventually he pulled his hands down from his face and said, "I'm having a harder and harder time getting around. I'm worried about the business. I've decided that I want to hurry up the process of selling. Why don't you invite Shyam, your father, and your math teacher to meet with us, so we can decide how to go about it? In the meantime I will talk to some of my banking friends about loans."

That was another surprise for Ram. Maybe he should mention Dashain now.

"There's no phone in the village," Ram started.

"Then how can you notify them?" his boss replied. "Obviously you depend on them for guidance."

"I would have to send a message or go up there myself. I could go during part of Dashain," Ram said hesitantly. "It starts next week."

Silence. The department managers stopped what they were doing and edged a little closer. The boss looked from one to the other of them, saying nothing. Then he turned towards Ram, looking him fully in the face. Ram met his gaze hopefully.

"We'll manage," said his boss. His color was better now and he seemed more in control of himself.

Now all the pieces of Ram's puzzle were on the table: Surya's demands to get him out of the house, the decision on his marriage, going back to the village for Dashain. buying the business. Would they fit together?

Chapter Twenty-Three

SHYAM

Chapter Twenty-Three

SHYAM

Shyam looked up from his carving. Dashain was beginning. He did not usually work during the holiday, but he had promised to finish carving the post for the tiny temple to *Durga Bhavani*, the goddess of strength and power, in time for worship there during Dashain. He and his father had installed the post first so the roofers could finish their work, and Shyam was having a hard time carving with the post since it was already in place.

He could not help but take a few moments to look at the beautiful day. It was crisp and cool here in the hills in mid-October. The sun shone brilliantly on the mountains across the valley, highlighting the white houses spread over the hillside. He could see the dome of the stupa outlined clearly at the top of the mountain. He had been up there once. The view had been spectacular. Beyond that mountain, the snow-covered Himalalya showed white with a few shadows of the deep crevasses. There was not a cloud in the azure sky.

Shyam took a deep breath as he considered his good fortune to be living and working in such a beautiful spot. He glanced around at some of the houses and thought with satisfaction of his part in constructing them. Then he looked back over the mountains again and thought of Ram and of their companionship over the years; their long talks, their sharing of dreams, and their mutual support. Shyam wondered if Ram was really content in his move to Kathmandu. He supposed they would be physically separated forever, but he missed having his brother around as a sounding board for his thoughts.

"Shyam! Shyam!" shouted Devi as she raced up the hill to where Shyam was working. "Ram's coming up the hill. Come on to meet him. He has surprised us coming home for Dashain!"

Shyam put down his tools as Devi grabbed his hand and pulled him down the hill. Ram was already at the house when they got there and so was Tara. Ram and Shyam looked with joy at each other. Their eyes sparkled and they laughed out loud as they clapped each other on the shoulder. In spite of their differences they still had a deep affection for one another.

"Now you two can slaughter the goat together for our feast," said Aama. "Baa has gone down the hill today to find a goat. We couldn't raise one this year. Dashain is so nice when families can get together."

Ram was had a hard time interrupting his mother, she was talking so fast. She paused when Sashi came in and stood shyly beside her. Ram went over and tried to pick her up, but Sashi twisted around and grabbed her mother.

"She has forgotten you already," said Shyam. "It has been a year since she saw you." Ram stared at his brother as he realized the truth in what he was saying. He could not believe it had been that long. "You are losing contact with your family," Shyam added. Ram nodded slightly as the two brothers maintained eye contact.

"I'll go and fix tea," said Aama. That was Aama's solution to awkward moments.

Just then Purna came in and bowed to his brother. Ram bowed in return, and then shook hands. Ram realized they would be entering into a new relationship; Purna was growing up, too.

"Purna, go get water for the tea and then go see if you can find your father. He can't have gone very far yet," said Aama. "Devi, you get mats for everyone to sit on and then come help with the tea."

Ram and Shyam went arm in arm to sit on the mat Devi spread for them. They were both smiling, seemingly determined not to let any differences come between them. Tara came over to sit beside Ram.

"Have you done anything about your plans for the store?" said Tara. "I bet your boss will stay there forever. Besides, I still think it's too big a place for you to manage. Kathmandu was so crowded. I was glad to get back to the village."

Ram was flattered that Tara was taking an interest in his plans, certainly more interest than Chandra took. Chandra never asked about his plans for his work. But, it was clear that Tara did not like Kathmandu. His thoughts started revolving again. He was glad he had the envelope from Surya. He did not know what the papers inside said, but maybe they would hold an answer to his marriage problem.

"Here comes the tea!" Devi exclaimed as she pranced ahead of her mother who was carrying the tea tray.

"And here comes the goat," said Baa as he came into the courtyard.

"She's cute!" said Sashi as she ran over and tried to pet it.

Shyam went to tie up the goat while Baa and Ram greeted one another. Ram took his tea. It was creamy and spicy just like he remembered it. He wondered if Tara made tea like that. Chandra's tea was good, he knew.

"Why did you bring the goat so early?" asked Shyam. "We won't need it for two weeks."

"It was too good a deal to pass up." replied Baa. Then he turned to Ram. "How long are you going to be here Ram? We need you to help paint the house again and slaughter the goat."

"I would like to do all of those things, but I can stay only a few days."

"But why?" said Baa and Aama and Shyam all at once.

Ram explained the problems with his boss.

"Well, then, we'll just have to have two feasts," said Aama. Baa wondered where they would get the money for another goat. Shyam wondered the same thing.

"Why don't we have chicken tomorrow to honor Ram," said Shyam. "We can fatten up the goat a little more and have it on the regular feast day."

"We'll have two chickens," said Aama as she counted the chickens pecking around the yard. "We will have a real feast. Shyam and Ram can each slaughter a chicken."

The next day was a beehive of activity as they prepared rice, lentils, cauliflower, beans, roti, and chicken curry. The roti was a special fried bread Ram's mother wanted to make for him. Everyone worked.

The weather was warm, so they sat on mats outside to eat. Aama carried around a pitcher of water to wash their hands. Then she and Devi served the food. All that could be heard for a while was the smacking of lips. Devi passed out more food under her mother's direction. *Devi is getting to be a big help,* thought Ram. *She is growing up, too.* He missed his family.

Ram withdrew the envelope from his pocket.

"I have some other things to share with you," began Ram. He emptied the contents and picked out Surya's letter. He decided he should read it out loud. In the letter Surya explained why he had taken on the role of match maker. He went on to describe the families he had talked with. Ram passed around the pictures. Chandra's was among them, Ram was relieved to see. Tara's name and picture were not. He supposed Surya had not even considered someone from the village.

Surya suggested that Ram's parents and brother come to Kathmandu to look for themselves. Baa, Aama, and Shyam looked bewildered. They had always thought Ram would return to the village to marry.

"There's another reason for you to come to Kathmandu and Bhaktapur," continued Ram. "As I said before, my boss is not very well. He wants to transfer his business to me soon. I need your advice, along with the math teacher's, about how to go about this. You are still my family and I want to know what you think is best."

There was complete silence.

"Why isn't anyone saying anything?" asked Devi.

Aama wiped her eyes. "I always thought Ram would marry someone close by and she would live with us and help with the farm."

"Ram is a good business man," said Baa. "He will earn money in Kathmandu and send it back to help us. We never have enough to buy the things we need. He needs a wife with him in Kathmandu. We will go to Kathmandu after Dashain to see for ourselves."

"I will always come home for Dashain," said Ram, in hopes of comforting his mother.

Shyam said nothing. He stared straight at the ground, trying to control his feelings. *I knew this was coming, but I don't know how I am going to be able to get along without Ram permanently*, he thought.

Aama went into the house to fix tea.

Chapter Twenty-Four

MHA PUJAA or HAPPY NEW YEAR

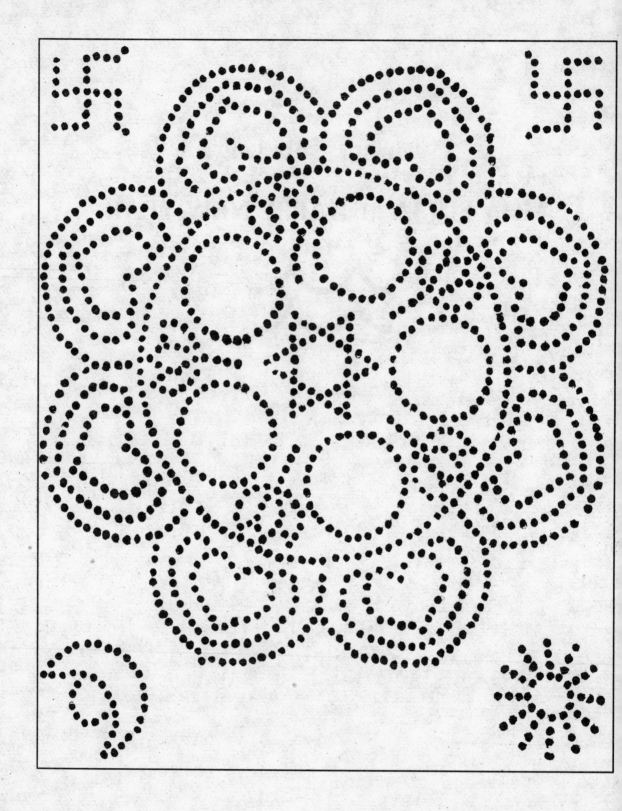

Chapter Twenty-Four

MHA PUJAA or HAPPY NEW YEAR

When is your family coming? Ram's boss, Mr. Tuladhar, asked a few days after Ram got back from the village.

"Soon, I hope," replied Ram. "They said they would come right after Dashain, but they might want to stay to celebrate the New Year. I hope they will be here for Tihar. Devi should be old enough to give me tika this year." Ram remembered the delicious experience of receiving his tika from Chandra last year.

When Ram had gotten back from the village, his boss welcomed him heartily. Ram was thankful that Mr. Tuladhar had recovered some of his old cheerfulness and seemed to be getting around a little better. He seemed frailer, though. His skin was almost transparent, his hair even whiter and thinner. It was obvious he was losing weight. Ram was anxious for his family to get here while his boss was able to handle the exchange of the store.

Ram let the managers go on holiday as promised. Due to the holiday. there was not much business, so he and his Mr. Tuladhar thought they could manage on their own. They closed the store only on the feast day. Mr. Tuladhar invited Ram him to celebrate with his family, but Ram thought he should not stay away from Surya's house. Now that he and Surya were not together all day, they got along better. Ram had not heard an *If you can't do it right...* in a long time. Surya was even acting as his surrogate father in choosing a bride for him. He hoped the matter would be settled soon.

A few days later was the Newar New Year. The year before he had missed the meal because he felt he would not be welcome. He was glad he would be included with Surya's family in the celebration this time. He hoped he would have a chance to see Chandra on that auspicious occasion but it did not work out that way.

Ram edged his way through the throngs and throngs of celebrants as he wove his way home from the bus stop. Stalls were set up all over the place, selling mostly food. The streets were filthy with trash, unusual for Bhaktapur. Between the trash and the crowds he was having a hard time finding a place to walk.

"Happy New Year," said a familiar voice. It was Surya.

"Happy New Year," shouted Ram in return. It was a merry scene.

Today was October 28, the first day of the Newar New Year for the year 1121. Other Nepali celebrated their New Year in April. This was the year 2057 for them. It was the year 2000 for westerners. Years counted for the Newars from the date when an enormous debt had been paid. It had been a miracle; a pile of sand had turned into gold.

Ram thought about his family who would be celebrating the day in his village. Maybe Tara would be there because the Newars usually got together for important dates. Ram had asked Surya about Tara for a bride. Surya gave an uncharacteristic shrug of his shoulders.

"Wait until your family gets here," Surya had replied.

Surya and Ram had become separated by the crowd, but arrived home about the same time. They took off their shoes and followed the children to a back room where more of Surya's family greeted them. Surya's mother was there, as was his sister. Both men bowed deeply to Surya's mother, stooping to touch her bare foot. Ram felt good about being included this time.

Small rugs, one for each person, lined two sides of the room. In front of each place was a colored rice powder mandala stenciled on the bare wooden floor. Marigold blossoms decorated the edges. A little rice and oil were at the center. Surya's mother took the first seat where she could see that the God received the offerings. Surya instructed each person to take a seat according to age. Surya sat next to his mother and then the others on around the wall down to his daughter at the end of the line.

As they sat down, Ram noticed some camphor, a little raw rice, and a small candle at each place. Surya's sister lit a piece of incense for everyone. Then she lit two wicks, about twenty centimeters long, for each person. If the wicks burnt off, it meant a short life. Ram watched with apprehension and fascination as his two wicks burned all the way to the end. He would have a long life.

He bit into a boiled duck egg and a fried fish Surya's sister gave him. The duck egg was a luxury. He found he liked it and ate it all, but he only nibbled at the fried fish. It was not very tasty. His family could not get fish often in the village. It was a long way down to the river for fish. He knew he should eat the crusty fish. Even at Surya's house, food was not wasted.

Next came a platter with fried vegetables and a leaf covered with beaten rice. There followed a parade of meats. Ram had never seen so much food or so many meats at one meal. Chicken, lamb, a meat patty, organ meats such as brain and tongue, and fat wrapped in skin, boiled and fried.

In all probability, his own family was eating various parts of a chicken, their only meat. Ram's grandmother, being the oldest at his house, was putting a tiny bit of each food on the ground for the gods, just as Surya's mother was doing.

At Surya's they served a series of drinks—Chang, the Nepali beer, the extra-strong Newar raksi, and finally tea. Then came the paan, the betal leaf wrapped around spices. Ram had not gotten used to the bits of green leaf that kept sticking to his teeth.

Ram worked his way through all these delicacies, but continued to think about his family whom he knew were having a much more modest feast. Mostly, he thought about Tara and Shyam. Tara had made an effort to talk to Ram when he was home, and did not show her past partiality to Shyam. Yet, Shyam seemed to show more interest in Tara, and he followed her with his eyes. *Do they talk together when I'm not around?* Ram wondered.

He looked at his watch. It was nearly midnight. They had been eating a long time. He said a silent prayer that the year 1121 would see his marriage and his new proprietorship. Some pieces of the puzzle were beginning to fit together.

Chapter Twenty-Five

BUSINESS AND BRIDES

Chapter Twenty-Five

BUSINESS AND BRIDES

Time dragged for Ram. Three weeks passed and still his family had not arrived. His boss asked him daily if he had heard from them. The boss did not seem to understand that there were no phones up there in the village. Ram agreed that his family at least could have sent a message. Surya was getting more edgy by the day. He wanted to get this business behind him and get Ram out of his house. Chandra was having a hard time knowing how to act. Surya had talked to her parents about the possibility of Ram's marriage to her. Chandra liked the idea and she thought her parents did, too. *Will I be a bride?* she wondered.

Suddenly, his mother and father, Shyam, and his math teacher appeared one evening at Surya's.

"What took you so long?" Ram asked, almost before finishing the customary greetings.

"We'll talk about that later," Baa replied. "First we need to get your business settled."

Three weeks of waiting for them, thought Ram, *and now they won't tell me why they were late.* But Ram knew he must respect what his father said. He telephoned his boss at home to say that his father, mother, math teacher and Shyam would be at the store in the morning.

Just as they got to the store, one of the managers arrived with a rack full of glasses of tea. Another manager was arranging chairs around a table covered with trays of sweets.

"Excuse me if I don't get up. My legs don't work so well any more," said the boss.

"Namaste!" said Ram's mother as she responded to the boss's bow. The others shook hands.

They were quiet for a while as they sipped tea. Ram and Shyam tried not to show their impatience.

"Have some cookies," said the boss as he pushed the trays toward them. Shyam and Ram were too much on edge to eat. The silence continued. Finally, Ram's father put down his tea cup.

"Ram's math teacher and Shyam have some new ideas which I am willing to support, but I think you should hear from them," Karna said.

The boss put his palms together, bowed slightly, and turned to the math teacher with a nod.

"Ram has told me a lot about your business and his work with Surya," began the math teacher. "He is anxious to put his own stamp on the business. I think it better that you hear from Shyam first as he has an idea how the business should operate."

Shyam bowed to the math teacher and to the boss. He explained his thoughts on a hardware store that would focus on the building trades.

"Our family has been doing wood construction for many years. Our caste have been woodcarvers from way back. I feel Ram should continue the tradition, combining it with his own merchandising talents."

"Ram has good organizational skills," the math teacher broke in. "When he worked for me he caught on quickly and turned into an expert merchandiser. He will do well." The math teacher leaned back and sipped his tea for a few minutes. "This sounds like an exciting project. I would like to continue to share ideas.

"Why not approach contractors in this area working on new buildings, such as hotels? I noticed several hotels under construction as we crossed the city. Now, I think Shyam should share some more of his thoughts."

"When I first came to Bhaktapur, I was overawed at the wood carvings done centuries back," Shyam began. "Later, as we passed through Kathmandu, I wondered at the buildings going up with such efficiency. I would like to know how this is done, what tools the workers use, and how they use them. I think you will sell more tools and materials if your sales people could provide instruction. Business focus and training are important."

The boss was quiet and serious for a while. Ram was holding his breath. *What if he doesn't like our ideas? What if he rejects them altogether?*

The silence did not last long.

"I have been impressed with this young man," the boss said as he looked at Ram. "He is young, though, and will need help. I am getting too old to lend the necessary guidance. I am ready to let Ram take over the store as soon as finances can be arranged. Already I have talked with two bank managers who might be interested in making the necessary loans. There is a provision, though. Shyam and the math teacher must stay here until their ideas are implemented, and they must come back periodically to see how the business is running. I will do what I can to keep an eye on things, but I will depend on you for consistent advice."

As soon as they got back to Bhaktapur after the meeting, Shyam grabbed Ram's arm.

"I want to go look again at the carvings in Durbar Square."

"Not now," Ram replied. "I want Aama and Baa to meet Chandra."

"That can wait," Shyam answered. "I must talk to you first."

Shyam and Ram threaded their way through the alleys, Shyam with his hands thrust in his pockets.

"What could be so serious that it could not wait?" asked Ram.

"I love Tara," Shyam blurted out.

Ram's face showed such a range of emotions that Shyam was not sure how his brother was taking this. At first it was shock as Ram felt his options cut off. Then it was questioning as he thought about what this meant for him and for Shyam. Then he grinned. They clapped each other on the back, and laughed. They were reading each other well once again. Nothing had to be said. The sun was beginning to set as they turned toward home.

"That is why we were so late getting here," said Shyam. "We wanted to make plans with Tara's family. The wedding will be within the next year, but I wanted to talk with you before we asked the priest to set the date. I knew you were interested in Tara, too."

"It has taken me all this time to realize how well-suited you and Tara are for each other," Ram said. "I was too busy thinking of myself." Ram and Shyam continued toward Surya's house arm in arm. It was almost dark when they headed across the square.

"We just met Chandra and her mother and father out in the square," said Maya.

"She's beautiful!" exclaimed Karna.

"She has nice manners," Aama said. "She would make a nice bride for you except that she won't be able to help us at home. I had hoped Ram would marry someone from the village so I would have two women to help me." Maya's eyes were brimming with tears.

"Now both of our boys will be married," said Baa. "Tara is a good worker and she will have to work extra hard. Surya has invited Chandra and her parents for dinner."

Maya composed herself. "I'll go help Surya's wife with the cooking. While I am in the kitchen I will fix tea."

Ram and Shyam smiled. Their mother had not changed. Tea was soothing.

"I can wear the new sari Ram bought me," Aama said as she left the room.

Miraculously enough, when Chandra's family came, everyone seemed to take it for granted that Chandra and Ram were going to be married. They would have to consult the priest about an auspicious date. Surya would host the wedding because the family would be in the village. Ram was elated, although he was afraid he and Surya might begin to have problems again. They might not agree about what were the right things to do for the wedding.

Chapter Twenty-Six

THE WEDDING

Chapter Twenty-Six

THE WEDDING

Shyam and the rest of Ram's family arrived a week ahead to help prepare for the wedding. Shyam and Ram were overwhelmed with all the preparations. Shyam knew the family would be doing it all again for him in a few months. Every other minute some new chore popped up.

"Ram, finish your tea quickly," said Surya. "We must go to the goldsmith's to pick up the bracelets for the bride. Everyone else must stay here to get everything ready to send to the bride's house this afternoon." The goldsmith met them at the store. The two bracelets were beautiful, about two centimeters wide with eight Buddhist good luck symbols in raised gold around them. The goldsmith carried the bracelets as he accompanied Surya and Ram back to the house.

It was a very long wait that first day, but finally everything was ready to send to the bride's house: a large pot decorated with good luck signs and filled with bread balls and small trinkets; a three tiered decorated cake; a large bowl of fruit; and a plate decorated like a cake with the name of Ram and Chandra. An urn of milk symbolized sending back the mother-in-law's milk that had been fed to her daughter while a baby. This urn was labeled with information about the wedding ceremonies. And then there were trays of items used in worship such as flowers, petals, and tika materials; a bowl of dried fish to bring good luck; a bowl of cloves; a red jacket for Chandra; silver ankle bracelets; and, of course, the golden bracelets. Everything was taken outside and loaded into a van to take to Chandra's house, accompanied by the goldsmith.

On the second day, Ram's excitement mounted. The wedding procession was about to go to Chandra's house to pick her up and bring her back. A band uniformed in red led the parade, followed by two men carrying large candles, another man carrying a pot with a wick, and then a man carrying two baskets filled with worship materials hanging from a rod across his shoulders. The car Shyam had helped decorate with tinsel took its place in line. Wedding guests followed, although most of the women stayed behind to get ready for the rest of the day. Ram watched from a balcony as Devi and Sashi took their places behind the car with the other girls. They were so cute in their frilly dresses! The men wore coats and ties. The parade went through the alleys to Durbar Square and then back around to Chandra's house.

Ram waited impatiently at home all day, although he understood that much of the ceremony went on at Chandra's house. Finally, late in the afternoon, the tinseled car drove up to Surya's front door. Chandra got out wearing a magnificent outfit. Her sari was red and gold brocade over a gold blouse. Gold bracelets covered each arm, and she wore rings on most fingers, many gold necklaces, and flowers in her hair. Ram looked down from the balcony above. She was beautiful, but he was dismayed that Chandra's head was down. She seemed sad and was crying. He watched patiently during the welcoming ceremonies as his mother washed Chandra's feet and sprinkled rice over her. Chandra held the main gate key as a sign of welcome. Ram put on his topi as Chandra came inside and they went to the back room to sit on large cushions with the priest. Chandra placed a wreath around Ram's neck and then walked three times around him. Surya helped Ram introduce the guests to Chandra.

When Ram and Shyam stepped out on the balcony early the next morning, the air was cool and fresh, a perfect day for the ceremony. After this Chandra and Ram would be considered husband and wife. But Shyam felt he had to take time out to look again at Durbar Square in the sunshine. Few people were around at that early hour. When he returned Chandra and Ram were seated on cushions. Shyam was almost late. It was his job to help place Ram's and Chandra's arms around each other, and lean their heads close together. Aama helped, too. The priest chanted.

Everyone got tika. Surya's sister passed curd for each person to dip a finger in and put on the temple, men on the right temple, women on the left. Duck eggs and fish came next. The raksi cups had to be filled three times as everyone ate with hands from leaf plates filled with food topped with yoghurt and sugar. A little food was thrown in front of the plates for the gods. Chandra and Ram had a platter with eighty-four types of food to be eaten with thumb and forefinger.

Surya outdid himself on the fourth day with the reception. He had rented a large hall and filled it with people. Ram's boss was there with his wife, the managers and their wives, and relatives and acquaintances of Surya's. Ram had the feeling that Surya might be practicing for the marriage of his own daughter. Chandra and her friends and family sat in a alcove where they could meet people and receive gifts. Ram could not settle down, but helped Surya make sure everything was running smoothly. Drinks and snacks, including chips and meatballs loaded with spices, kept coming. Shyam was enjoying himself, particularly the buffet where he could eat as much as he wanted. He and Ram and Baa sat together for a short while.

"I'm glad tomorrow is an almost off day," said Ram. "These four days have been fun, but I am exhausted. I'm glad Chandra can raise her head to look at people sometimes. Why must brides appear so sad? Do you think she is that unhappy about leaving her parents' home and living a new life?"

"All brides do that," said Baa. "In Chandra's case, she must be pretending."

The last day, two days later, was the longest of all. In a corner, the priest and Ram sat cross-legged on the floor across from each other for nearly an hour doing worship ceremonies such as lighting incense, making offerings, and even starting a small fire for offerings. A little Buddhist alter was set up at one side. Ram looked up and saw men coming in with a parade of gifts similar to the ones Ram's family had sent to Chandra's house. Bric-a-brac. Clothes. Toiletries. A silver tray full of silver items. Rice powder for the face, comb and brush, red powder and silver combs for the hair.

When Chandra entered, she and Ram stood in the middle of a swastika, an auspicious symbol in the East, drawn on the floor. Surya's sister gave them tika. They made an offering and took their positions on their cushions. The priest was working with them using incense and tapers, and ringing the bell periodically. It seemed the ceremonies took on more religious aspects as the day went on.

Ram was glad when the tone changed to the ceremony of dressing the bride by the groom. It was fun.

He got to stick combs and flowers and bows in Chandra's hair. He took a long string and wound it through the five buns in her hair and then tried to apply cosmetics. It was hard with Chandra's head down. Ram thought he heard her laughing. In return Chandra put some Bryl Cream in his hair. Cameras clicked and the camcorder rolled. Chandra and Ram went out on the balcony to make an offering to a statue of Ganesh, the elephant god.

After a short rest everyone got ready to go to the temple, a small one close to Swayambu. Ram and Shyam had walked the 308 steps up to the Swayambu stupa several times in the past week to get away from the preparations. They felt much calmer after pausing at the Buddha and then turning the prayer wheels as they walked around the stupa. The temple Ram and Chandra used was an old one with a pagoda at one corner, and a courtyard filled with several stone chortens celebrating the lives of loved ones.

The wedding continued as the priest put red powder in Chandra's hair, signifying she was a married woman. Surya's sister gave everyone a red tika and a black tika, signifying extra good luck. And then, of course, there was another meal beginning with duck eggs, dried fish, and beaten rice. Ram and Chandra were getting their second wind as they joked and laughed with the guests.

One more hurdle. Chandra went back to her house accompanied by the men in the family. Chandra's family would have a chance to see that she was still all right after six days of wedding. Chandra was queen then, sitting on a couch receiving gifts of saris and money from the men. She looked eagerly for Ram. It had been a long day with several other long days before that. She was anxious to get to the apartment that she and Ram had rented. It was time to get on with their lives.

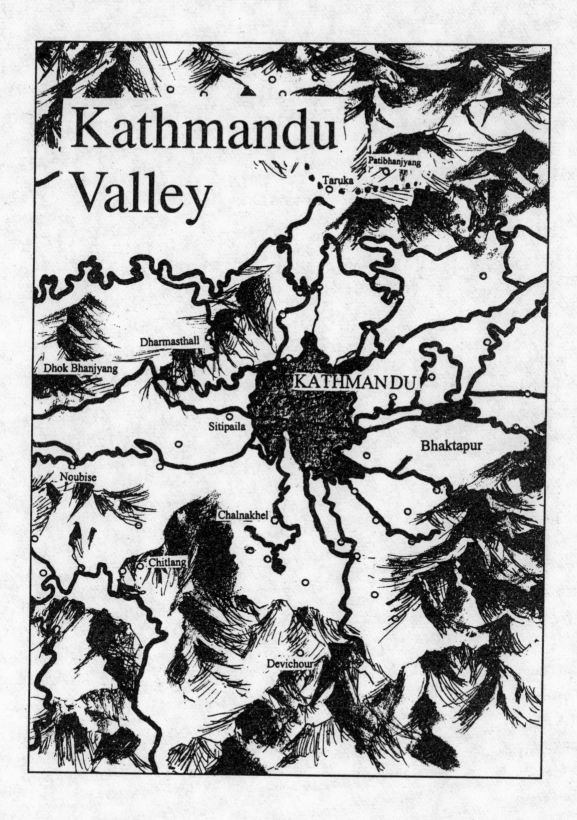

MORE FOLK TALES
FROM PILGIRMS PUBLISHING

www.pilgrimsbooks.com

For catalog and more information mail or fax to:

PILGRIMS BOOK HOUSE

Mail Order, P. O. Box 3872, Kathmandu, Nepal
Tel: 977-1-424942 Fax: 977-1-424943
E-mail: mailorder@pilgrims.wlink.com.np

Printed in India at Excel Prints, N. Delhi-28. Ph. 5893485